High Trail to Danger

High Trail
to Danger

◆ ◆ ◆

Joan Lowery Nixon

BANTAM BOOKS
NEW YORK • TORONTO • LONDON • SYDNEY • AUCKLAND

HIGH TRAIL TO DANGER

A Bantam Book / June 1991

*The Starfire logo is a registered trademark of Bantam
Books, a division of Bantam Doubleday Dell Publishing
Group, Inc. Registered in U.S. Patent
and Trademark offices and elsewhere.*

Library of Congress Cataloging-in-Publication Data

Nixon, Joan Lowery.
    High trail to danger / Joan Lowery Nixon.
      p.   cm.
    Summary: In 1879 seventeen-year-old Sarah travels
from Chicago to the violent town of Leadtown, Colorado,
to locate her missing father, but she finds that the mention
of his name brings her strange looks and an attempt on
her life.
    ISBN 0-553-07314-1
    [1. West (U.S.)—Fiction. 2. Colorado—Fiction. 3. Mystery
and detective stories.] I. Title.
PZ7.N65Hi   1991
[Fic]—dc20
                               90-20072
                                     CIP
                                     AC

PRINTED IN THE UNITED STATES OF AMERICA

BVG   0 9 8 7 6 5 4 3 2 1

Chapter 1

◆　　◆　　◆

At the rooster's crow Sarah struggled from a comforting swirl of dreams into a dark gray, needle-sharp morning. She flung out an arm, mumbling, "Don't leave us!"

"Ouch!" Her younger sister, Susannah, wiggled free of the tangled sheet, pushed away Sarah's arm, and muttered, "Sarah! Wake up!"

"I am awake." As Sarah swung her feet over the side of the bed, tears rose to her eyes. "I was dreaming about Mother. There's a great, gaping hole inside of me. You understand what I mean, don't you? It's like the blackness when you look beyond the stars. Or like . . ."

"Sarah," Susannah interrupted, "I do *not* understand. You're the one who turns words into pictures in your head. I'm like Mother—like Mother was. I say what I think in plain English." She scrambled from the bed and lit a candle before she pulled off her cotton shift. "And I don't try to hide behind words the way you sometimes do."

"I don't try to hide behind them!" Sarah insisted, but

she hunched her shoulders and wished she could spin the moonlight into a magic coverlet that would protect them both and transport them back to the time before Mother grew so ill. She closed her eyes, trying to visualize a happier time, but the only image she saw was that of the marker at the head of her mother's grave: Margaret Alicia Lindley, born April 3, 1841; died August 15, 1879. As plainly as though her mother had said it, the words came into Sarah's head: *There is no going back.*

"I can't believe she's gone," Sarah murmured.

"Sarah, Mother's dead," Susannah said. "We have to accept it. There are important things we'll have to do." A floorboard creaked in the hall, and Susannah whispered, "We'll talk about it all later. Hurry! You know they'll be angry if we're late!"

Sarah nodded. Since Uncle Amos and Aunt Cora had moved in, taking over the boardinghouse as though they had the right to do so, Sarah and Susannah were kept hard at work every moment of the day.

Dressing by candlelight, Sarah poured water from the pitcher into the bowl and scrubbed at her face. With just a few strokes of her hairbrush, she smoothed her long, dark auburn hair, coiling it into a twist at the back of her head and anchoring it with large amber hairpins. Her bangs and the short locks that framed her face curled naturally, softening the hollows under her cheekbones and heightening her long, dark lashes.

Sarah quickly pulled the strings of the corset she wore over her pantaloons and chemise, and when her waist was nipped in as tightly as possible, she fastened the strings. Next she pulled on long, white cotton stockings and fastened them to the garter straps on the corset. She stepped into a full cotton petticoat, a light blue chambray skirt, and a plain, short-sleeved, white cotton blouse, then bent to tug on high-topped shoes, which were fastened with a row of tiny buttons.

After making a quick trip to the backyard privy and washing her hands in a bowl on the screened-in porch off the kitchen, Sarah finally was ready to light the fire in the stove and the oil lamps for the kitchen and dining room and begin preparations for breakfast.

By this time Susannah had joined her, her thin cotton dress loosely hanging from her shoulders to the calves of her legs over a sturdy white muslin petticoat. Sarah saw that Susannah's long, black cotton stockings were wrinkled, and she smiled. Susannah thought of herself as practical, like their mother, but she was still just a girl. She loved to go barefoot in the heat and hated the stockings. She rarely tried to fasten them properly.

Susannah ran outside to collect the hens' fresh eggs. It would also be her job to cut thick slices of the bread they'd baked the afternoon before.

Sarah poured about a half cup of pork grease into a large iron skillet. As it began to heat, she sliced raw potatoes into the pan, watching droplets from the slices jump and spit and sizzle.

"Here, here!" Cora spoke from behind her, startling Sarah. "Go easy on the potatoes. You don't have to use that many."

"Mother always told us, one potato per person."

Cora's nasal voice twanged with impatience. "It doesn't matter what Margaret said. She spent too much money—

apparently as much as she earned." Her eyes narrowed as she studied Sarah. "Unless things aren't quite what they seem to be around here."

Sarah stared back at her pinched-face aunt. What was the matter with Uncle Amos and Aunt Cora? Why this preoccupation with money? Mother's brother and his wife had arrived during Mother's last days, had stayed to help—as they'd put it—and had immediately taken possession of the house, everything in it, and Mother's bank account as soon as Mother died.

It had occurred to Sarah that Mother may have kept some money around the house, but she had soon rejected the idea. If there had been a few dollars extra tucked away among Mother's personal things, Uncle Amos and Aunt Cora would have found them.

Sarah was satisfied in seeing Aunt Cora's glance falter, but as Cora looked away, she snapped, "From now on there'll be chops or sausage only three times a week—Tuesday, Thursday, and Sunday—and a limit of one egg per person per day. That's certainly enough."

"But the men won't be happy if they don't get meat with breakfast, and Mr. Abrams always eats three eggs."

"If they don't care for the way we do things, they can go somewhere else, and we'll get folks here who are more easily satisfied," Cora said. She turned her back on Sarah and set about filling the tiny crystal salt cellars that would be placed at each end of the large dining table.

Sarah fought back her anger and returned to her work. She hoped Mr. Abrams wouldn't move away. He was a jolly, grandfatherly clothing salesman with muttonchop whiskers, twinkling eyes, and a ready smile.

He'd been with them longer than any of the other boarders, and he'd always been happy.

Besides the fine meals Mother had always served, she'd created an attractive home. The spotless lace curtains at the windows, the deep, red plush-covered sofas and chairs, the comfortable beds with their white cotton spreads, the velvet pillows with fringe and tassels, the hand-painted bowls always filled with fruit in the summer and nuts for cracking in the winter, and the scenic landscape prints in their ornate frames helped make the Lindleys' boardinghouse a favorite, and rarely had there been an empty room.

Sarah heard two deep voices in the dining room and checked the time. Almost six o'clock.

As she carried in the plates, roly-poly, gray-haired Mr. Abrams beamed up at her. "A very good morning to you, Sarah," he said.

Sarah smiled back. "And a good morning to you."

But as she took a step toward the kitchen, Mr. Abrams reached out and clasped her wrist. "Sarah," he murmured, "I have eyes and ears, and I do not like what I see and hear in this house. I have talked with Susannah. I will help." He let go of her wrist and began to eat as though their conversation had never taken place.

What did he mean by that? Sarah wondered, but another boarder had arrived in the dining room, and there was no time left to think about it.

Finally, with everyone served and the table cleared, Sarah and Susannah sat at the kitchen table, ready to eat their own meal. Aunt Cora usually gave them a few moments to eat in peace, but today Uncle Amos pulled out a chair opposite them and sat down. His nose was as beaked and his jowls as dark and flaccid as the backyard rooster's. He leaned his forearms on the table, laced his fingers together, and stared from one girl to the other without saying a word.

Sarah began to feel more and more uneasy under his stare. She dropped a piece of buttered bread, then a few moments later choked on a bite of egg, gasping while Susannah pounded on her back.

As Sarah sipped some water and tried to breathe normally, Susannah spoke up. "What do you want, Uncle Amos?"

"You know what I want," he said. "Somewhere in this house there's money hid. Margaret had a hiding place, and you know where it is."

"That's not true!" Normally Sarah would not have lost her patience, but she was tired of her uncle and aunt's false accusations.

"Isn't it?" Uncle Amos leaned toward them, scowling, and Sarah pressed against the back of her chair. "I can add two and two, girlie," he said. "While your mother was abed, there were no bank deposits made. Two months or more that was, yet records show that all the boarders paid on time each week. So where'd that money go to?"

"I—I don't know," Sarah stammered. "If Mother had a hiding place, she didn't tell us about it. I have no idea where one could be."

From the corner of her eye, she saw Susannah pick up her fork and calmly take a large bite of potato.

"How about you, then?" Uncle Amos shifted his attention to Susannah.

6

Susannah continued to chew slowly. Uncle Amos's eyebrows drew together in a deep frown. "I asked you a question," he said.

Sarah put a hand on Susannah's arm. "Don't be angry, Uncle Amos. Her mouth is full, and she can't answer yet." Even though Sarah was terrified by this man and how he might react to her boldness, she continued, "I'm older. If Mother had a secret to share, she'd tell *me*, wouldn't she? Not Susannah. If there is a secret hiding place in this house, we don't know anything about it and can't even guess where it might be."

Uncle Amos shoved back his chair, scraping the bare floorboards with a rasping whine. "Then we'll have to begin a search," he said. "If no hiding place happens to turn up before tomorrow morning, we'll take each room apart, board by board, until we find it." He stood up, towering over them, and added, "We'll begin with your room."

As he and Cora left the kitchen, Sarah turned to her sister. "He means it," she said.

"I know." Susannah's expression was somber, but she calmly continued eating.

Sarah drew back and studied Susannah. It wasn't just that Susannah behaved like Mother, so practical and plainspoken. She even looked more like their mother than Sarah did. While Sarah was tall and slender with long fingers, dark auburn hair, and soft hazel eyes, Susannah had the same dark brown eyes and light hair, the same small, compact, no-nonsense build as their mother. At fourteen—close to fifteen—Susannah had already begun to mature, and soon she'd be a beauty.

Mother had seen it, too. "Susannah's like me," she'd

say proudly, giving her youngest daughter a special glance. But her smile would turn rueful as she'd playfully pat Sarah's cheek and add, "Sarah, now, takes after her father—both of them dreamers and always will be."

Sarah loved her books, her music, and the poetry she secretly wrote by candlelight, but she never neglected her work. She wished that Mother would compliment her just once on never stinting in her household tasks, on always helping to keep spotless every room in the boardinghouse. But Mother wasn't one to give compliments and praise. Her daughters were simply expected to do a good job with whatever tasks were given them and be glad they'd done them well.

And Mother hadn't meant to be unkind when she'd compared Sarah to her father. Sarah was aware that Mother had never stopped loving him. Mother had saved his infrequent letters, tying them in small bundles with narrow lengths of satin ribbon that were frayed from being tied and untied so often.

Once Sarah had come upon her mother reading the letters. Mother had looked up with a guilty smile, clutched the packet more firmly, and murmured, "I hope you girls don't hold hard thoughts about your father. In spite of his faults, Benjamin was always a kind, loving man."

"Where is he, Mother?" Sarah had asked. For a while after he had left them, Sarah had often pulled the quilt over her head and wept silently in the night, aching because she and Mother and Susannah had been abandoned by this wonderful, mischief-loving father with the eyes that sparkled and the lips from which wondrous stories flowed. She had loved the poems he'd read to her—Lord Byron's, John Keats's, Percy Shelley's. Why had Father gone? Hadn't he loved his wife and daughters as much as they had loved him?

But ten years was a long time, and now she rarely thought of Father at all.

Mother had sat upright in the rocking chair, firmly tying the ribbon with a no-nonsense knot. "Last I heard, a year ago December," she'd answered, "Ben had left Denver and was trying his luck in some little mining town."

"*Sarah!*" Susannah hissed. "Stop daydreaming and come outside with me quickly—behind the chicken coop! They won't look for us for a few minutes."

As Sarah followed Susannah to a shaded place behind the chicken coop, Susannah whispered, "I told you, there are important things we have to do. After what Uncle Amos said this morning, they're even more important."

When Susannah had this determined look in her eye, it was best and easiest just to listen to what she had to say. "Tell me," Sarah said.

"We can't allow Uncle Amos and Aunt Cora to take everything away from us. We have rights."

"What rights? We're girls, and we're not old enough to provide for ourselves. What Mother had belongs to Father, not to us."

"They weren't thinking about Father when they took over our boardinghouse."

"They haven't exactly taken it over. They're working to keep the boardinghouse going. It's our livelihood."

"It's become *their* livelihood," Susannah insisted. "It's *their* boardinghouse, run *their* way. They're in Mother's room, even using Mother's things." Her voice broke, and she swallowed hard before she continued. "Mother's favorite silver-and-garnet pin—the one Father gave her—didn't you notice yesterday evening? Aunt Cora was wearing it!"

Sarah hadn't noticed, and she was shocked. "I told Aunt Cora that Mother had said the pin would someday be yours. Aunt Cora told me she had searched and couldn't find it."

"Did you believe her?"

"I didn't know what to believe. Aunt Cora told me that Mother had probably put it away for safety in a secret hiding place. She said she would go with me to the hiding place to look for it, but I told her I didn't know of any such place."

Susannah scowled. "She tried that trick on me, too. Maybe wearing the pin was her way of showing us that she was determined to find the hiding place in spite of us."

"But there *isn't* a hiding place," Sarah insisted.

"Yes, there is," Susannah said. "I walked in on Mother one day when she had removed a short section of loose floorboard behind her bed. There's a hollow there, between the floor and the ceiling."

Sarah was stunned. She had told Uncle Amos in all honesty that there wasn't such a place. "But what was she hiding?" Sarah asked. "Mother had no real valuables."

"It was a place to keep the money the boarders paid each week until she could get to the bank. And it was a place to keep extra money—some cash on hand in case of emergencies." Susannah paused and lowered her voice. "I promised Mother I would never tell anyone, and I didn't, not even you. Please don't be angry with me."

"I could never be angry with you," Sarah said, though she had to fight back the hurt that tightened her throat.

"Listen," Susannah whispered, "I used the hiding place to stash the money the boarders paid while Mother was ill, and I added to it the rest of the greenbacks that were there, so we'll have enough."

Sarah was bewildered. "Enough for what?"

"Enough for you to go west and find Father and bring him home."

Sarah staggered back a step, almost losing her balance. "W-what?" she stammered.

"You heard me!" Susannah grabbed Sarah's hands. "You have to go. Don't you see? The house and everything in it belongs to *us*, not to Uncle Amos and Aunt Cora. It belongs to Father, too."

"Well, yes, but . . ."

"And Father should be told about Mother."

Sarah nodded. It hadn't occurred to her. "Yes," she said. "We'll need to tell Father, but we could just write to him, couldn't we?"

"We aren't sure where he is. The last address on the letters he sent Mother was Leadville, Colorado. He's probably working in the silver mines near there. A letter sent to him care of Leadville general delivery could sit waiting for him for months—even years. But if you go to Leadville, and Father has moved on, there's sure to be someone who'll know where he's gone and who can send you in the right direction."

Sarah took a deep breath. "How can I go after Father?" she asked. "Colorado is such a long distance from

Chicago. A woman traveling alone . . . There'd be dangers. . . . What about outlaws? And Indians? Are there Indians?"

"Listen," Susannah said. "I asked Mr. Abrams for help, because I knew he wouldn't tell. Mr. Abrams said that Leadville is a mining town, up in the Colorado mountains. From Chicago to Denver people travel by train, from Denver to Leadville by stagecoach."

A sudden thought gave Sarah a burst of hope. "Susannah, you'd be so much better at making the trip than I would. You're the practical one. You'd know what to do."

"Yes, I wish I could go." Susannah grimaced. "But I'm too young. You're seventeen. Old enough to come and go as you please without question."

"Come with me."

Susannah shook her head. "There's only enough money for one person to make the trip, along with Father's fare back. Mr. Abrams brought me a railway schedule, and he figured what other expenses you'd have along the way."

"I can't leave you here with Uncle Amos and Aunt Cora."

Susannah's voice was firm and insistent. "Of course you can. They are disagreeable and small-minded and mean-hearted, but they won't do me any physical harm. I'll take care of myself while you're gone."

"You're not afraid?"

"No, I'm not."

Sarah moaned. "But I am. I'm terrified, Susannah."

"I know that," Susannah said, "but you'll stop being terrified after you're on the way. It will be an adventure!"

"I'll see Father again," Sarah said slowly. Once more she'd bask in his smile and the happy twinkle in his eyes. "He will come back with me, Susannah. In his own way he loves us."

Susannah put a hand on her arm. "Think about Father later. We haven't time to talk any longer." She tugged a tightly wrapped packet from the deep pocket of her dress and handed it to Sarah. "Here's the money. Tuck it inside your bodice, where it will be safe. I've found a carpetbag in the attic and hidden it under the bed, and I'll help you pack. There's a train for Denver leaving the Chicago railway station at four P.M., and you're going to be on it."

Chapter 2

◆　　◆　　◆

Sarah tiptoed into the house and fled up the stairs. The money! No matter where she hid it in the room, Uncle Amos would find it. She'd have to keep it on her person.

Carefully she loosened her corset, tucked the packet in at the top, and pulled the strings together again. The packet pressed so tightly against her ribs that it was hard to take a deep breath, but at least it was secure. The rest of the day, as Sarah scrubbed and polished, she willed herself not to think about leaving Chicago. Over and over she'd read in newspaper accounts and dime novels chilling tales about the wild—the *very* wild— West. How could she face those terrors alone, without protection? She had promised to go, she had accepted the need to go, but she didn't want to think about it. Not yet.

Close to two in the afternoon, Susannah waylaid Sarah as she passed through the screened porch. "As usual Uncle Amos left on 'business,' and Aunt

Cora went upstairs to nap. Now, Sarah. Now it's time to go!"

Susannah tugged Sarah up the stairs, both girls wincing at each creak and pop of the boards, and led her into the bedroom. As soon as the door was closed, she pulled a shabby carpetbag, left behind by a former boarder, from under the bed.

"I've packed everything you'll need, including your coat," Susannah told her. "Denver's altitude is high, and Leadville even higher. Late September is already early winter there."

Sarah's expression must have mirrored her fear. "Believe in yourself, Sarah," Susannah urged. "You have to be positive that you can do anything you set your mind to."

"It's not that easy," Sarah said.

Susannah gave Sarah a reassuring hug. "You'll go to Leadville, you'll find Father, and you'll be back with him in no time, so stop worrying. Now change your clothes. Be quick about it. I've laid out a shirtwaist and skirt that are sturdy enough for travel."

As Sarah dressed, she suddenly remembered. "The money," she said. "It's all in my corset."

"The corset is a good place to keep it," Susannah told her. "It could be stolen from the carpetbag." Her voice low, Susannah cautioned, "You are always too trusting of people. Keep in mind there are unscrupulous people about. If the money's safely hidden on your person, all to the good."

She reached under the quilt on the bed and pulled out a small drawstring purse made of black serge and embroidered with black silk thread. "Here's Mother's reticule. Put only the money you think you will need each day in this, and keep the rest in the packet tucked inside your corset. In addition to the amount you'll need for your train fare, the purse already has enough in it to pay your expenses for a few days."

Sarah drew the cords of the reticule tight and looped them over her left arm, while Susannah picked up the carpetbag and walked out the bedroom door. As silently as possible Sarah crept downstairs following Susannah, clutching the stair rail for support. At the foot of the stairs, she stopped in front of the narrow mirror, with its gilt frame of cupids and flower swags, to smooth back a few tendrils of hair that curled over her ears. She lifted a gray felt bonnet from the nearby hat rack and anchored it by pushing the four-inch pin snugly through the thick, tautly held hair on top of her head. Mother had given Sarah the hat last winter, decorating it herself with a bright peacock blue ribbon, which Sarah tied in a bow under her chin.

Will this be the last time I'll see myself in this mirror? Will I ever come home again? Sarah asked herself. For a moment she felt dizzy.

"Don't take such pains with that bow!" Susannah whispered. She noiselessly opened the front door and stepped outside. As they reached the street, Susannah suddenly threw her arms around Sarah and held her tightly. "I'll miss you!" she said, her voice rough with tears. "Oh, how I'll miss you! Hurry back, Sarah."

Sarah hugged Susannah in return. "How can I go? I can't! I can't leave you, Susannah! I can't face that awful unknown country! I can't . . ."

Susannah interrupted Sarah by twisting away, grabbing her sister's shoulders, and giving them a firm shake. "Stop it!" she said. "No more letting down. We *both* have to be brave." Once more Susannah had become the strong sister.

"But I'm not."

"You can be just as brave as I can be, Sarah Ann Lindley. If you haven't discovered what's inside you, then you'll just have to take my word for it." Susannah bent down and picked up the carpetbag, thrusting it into Sarah's hands. She nodded at a cab and driver that waited down near the corner. "Mr. Abrams arranged for the cab. The driver's waiting to take you to the station, and don't give him a penny, because he's already been paid."

"Susannah, I . . ."

Susannah took a step backward, her lips tight. "No more good-byes, Sarah. Go! Hurry, or Uncle Amos will be back and we'll lose everything!"

But Sarah hesitated. "Thank Mr. Abrams for me. Tell him to watch over you until Father and I return."

"He will. Sarah! Go!"

Gripping the heavy bag as tightly as she could, Sarah ran toward the cab. "To the railway station, please," she said to the driver, who was perched on a high seat above the cab. Sarah climbed in and shut the door, and as the driver clucked to the horses and the cab began moving with a jolt, she rested her head against the high-backed seat and tried to think.

What am I doing? What's going to become of Susannah and me? Sarah waited for an answer to come to her, but none did. She could still see her sister's face, tears

17

welling in Susannah's deep brown eyes in spite of her brave pose. No longer able to hold back her own loneliness and fear, Sarah burst into tears.

Cabs, horse-drawn trucks, and pedestrians swarmed outside the railway station, an imposing building decorated with tall, ornate pillars and a high-domed roof. Sarah's cab stopped with a jerk that nearly sent her sprawling. She pulled herself together as the driver reached down and threw open the cab door.

"Here you be, miss," he said.

Sarah gripped her carpetbag and climbed from the cab, wishing she could put her hands over her ears to shut out the noise.

Horses' hooves smacked the pavement, wagon wheels creaked, voices called to each other. Someone was shouting. . . .

Strong hands gripped Sarah's shoulders, nearly lifting her from her feet, as she was rushed across the street and deposited on the pavement in front of the station's doors.

"You nearly got run over. Don't you know you're not supposed to stand in the street, gawking?"

Sarah, pink with embarrassment, looked up into the shining brown eyes of a young man who was probably less than a half dozen years older than she. He was tall and trim in a fashionable high-buttoned brown travel suit with a ticket pocket over the right-hand pocket of the single-breasted coat.

As the smile in his eyes spread to his lips, Sarah mumbled, "Please don't laugh at me!"

"I'm not laughing," he answered.

She realized that he was studying her appreciatively, and she blushed even more furiously.

"Look back there," he said, motioning toward the street. "See that big dray being pulled by the Percherons? The driver was yelling at you to get out of the way. He wouldn't have been able to stop his team in time. Thanks to my being on hand, you're still in one piece."

"T-thank you," Sarah stammered, wishing she could think of exactly the right thing to say.

He swept off the cap he was wearing and made a little bow, his short, light brown hair almost blond in the sunlight. "May I introduce myself? My name is Jeremy Caulfield."

Sarah took a step backward as Susannah's warnings came to mind. The simple rules of proper behavior made it clear that she had no business speaking to a stranger in public, even though that stranger was very handsome, and even though he had saved her life.

"Mr. Caulfield," she said formally, "I shall always be grateful to you for rescuing me. Now please excuse me." Sarah turned her back on Jeremy, shifted the heavy bag to her right hand, and walked as fast as she could into the main building of the railway station.

People were everywhere, some of them shoving against each other. Two well-dressed women accompanied by men wearing tailored suits and formal high hats made their way through the crowd by carrying parasols in front of them like weapons. The noise of hundreds of voices echoing in the vast room beat against Sarah's ears, and for a moment she closed her eyes, wanting to blot it all out, wishing she could find herself back in her own house with Susannah and Mother. Sarah struggled through the pushing, hurrying travelers. Where was the train? Where should she buy her ticket? What was she doing here?

"Carry your bag, lady?"

Sarah looked down to see a ragged, dirty-faced boy who was no taller than her waist. He grinned as his fingers squirmed next to hers on the handle of the bag.

"Why, thank you," Sarah began, but a hand grabbed the neck of the boy's shirt and lifted him off his feet.

"Get out of here, you scallywag," Jeremy said, "or I'll turn you over to a policeman!"

Cursing, the boy squirmed free, dived into the crowd, and immediately disappeared.

"He would have made off with your satchel," Jeremy told Sarah.

"I suppose you think I'm totally incompetent," Sarah snapped, her embarrassment causing her to blush again. She had to be honest with herself. She was glad to see Jeremy Caulfield, and she was glad he had stepped in to save her.

"I'm sorry," Jeremy said as he leaned forward. "Your voice is very soft—beautiful, too—and I couldn't hear what you said to me."

Sarah relaxed and smiled. "I said, thank you," she shouted.

The teasing sparkle in Jeremy's smile made Sarah think of Father's smile, and her heart gave a little jump.

"Do you have your ticket?" Jeremy asked. As Sarah shook her head, he added, "Then may I help you get it?"

It would be so easy just to turn everything over to this kind gentleman, but Sarah resisted the temptation.

Since she was going to make the trip west alone, she would have to learn from the start to handle problems herself, and so far she hadn't made a very good beginning.

"Just tell me, please, where I should purchase my ticket," she said shyly.

He bent an elbow, inviting Sarah to take his arm, and said, "Come with me. I'll take you there."

But Susannah's warning flashed into Sarah's mind again. Jeremy was charming—maybe too charming. In spite of his introduction, he was a stranger, and they had not been properly introduced.

Jeremy had taken a step toward the right as he gave his invitation. Sarah smiled graciously and said, as loudly as she could, "Thank you very much for your help, Mr. Caulfield, but it would not be proper for me to take up any more of your time."

Quickly glancing away from the amusement in his eyes, she strode off toward the right and soon found a row of windows through which agents were selling railway tickets. Sarah stood behind a large, authoritative gentleman, who soon concluded his business, and stepped up to one of the barred windows.

"Where to?" the ticket agent growled, his voice bristling like his heavy moustache.

Unable to answer now that the moment had come, Sarah stood as erect as she could and forced herself to breathe evenly. "Leadville, Colorado," she finally managed to say.

The agent leaned toward her, poking his face near the bars of the window, and scowled. "The trains don't go to Leadville."

Sarah remembered what Susannah had told her.

"Oh, that's right. Denver, please. I need a ticket to Denver."

"Make up your mind. I can route you Chicago to St. Louis, St. Louis to Kansas City, Kansas City to Denver. If you want that, fine. If you don't, then step aside. There's folks lined up behind you."

Who did this man think he was to talk to her like that! Sarah would have liked to tell him that he should be ashamed of himself for being so rude, but when she opened her mouth, only a timid whisper came out. "Please . . . I want a coach ticket to Denver."

"That'll be twenty dollars." The agent pulled some slips of printed pasteboard from a drawer, pounded them with the inked stamp in his fist, and handed them across to Sarah. She opened the drawstrings on her purse and pulled out the bills inside, counting out the correct amount. A little frightened because such a small amount of money was left in the reticule, Sarah accepted the tickets, tucking them into the purse. At this rate it seemed unlikely that the money securely fastened inside her corset really would be enough to take her the rest of the way to Leadville and home again to Chicago.

The agent was speaking, and Sarah tried to concentrate. "You go through this big room to the train shed," the agent told her, "and there'll be conductors there to direct you to the train to St. Louis. It's already in the shed, and you can board."

"Thank you," Sarah said. She hefted her bag and strode briskly through the huge, domed room toward the train shed.

A conductor in uniform studied Sarah's tickets and directed her to one of the cars on the nearest train. He helped her with her bag, shoving it under one of the empty seats before he trotted back to the platform to aid other travelers.

Sarah's legs wobbled as she plopped down into the seat and slid over to the side by the window. She had actually come this far. She was on the train, on her way to find her father.

The curtains at the window were held back with small ties at each side so that Sarah had a clear view of the shed, with its arched network of metal supports, which reminded her of a giant spiderweb, and the crowd that milled through the station. Nervously she studied the faces and prayed that Uncle Amos wouldn't have learned yet that she had gone. Surely he'd come to the station after her.

Sarah was not aware that someone had sat down next to her and stowed his bag beside hers until he spoke.

"How far will you be traveling? Missouri? Kansas?"

Sarah whirled at the sound of the familiar voice. "Mr. Caulfield," she asked, "are you following me?"

Jeremy's face grew serious. "I wish I were," he said. "But, unfortunately, I have no choice about where I'll be traveling."

Sarah, who didn't know what to answer, turned back to the window to cover her confusion. What should she do now? It wouldn't be proper to converse with a stranger, no matter what the circumstances. Yet if they were traveling together, how could they avoid speaking?

I'll be reserved, she thought. *Friendly, yet proper.* Satisfied with her decision, she again stared out at the people milling through the train shed.

A tall man with stooped shoulders passed nearby, and Sarah stiffened. He turned, and she caught a quick glimpse of dark jowls and a beaked nose. With a smothered cry Sarah pressed back against the side of the coach.

Chapter 3

.   .   .

"What is it?" Jeremy leaned toward Sarah. "Why are you so frightened?" His voice was kind, and his eyes were filled with concern.

Forget propriety! Close to panic Sarah blurted out, "Just outside the train . . . my uncle . . ." But she sneaked another fearful look and saw that the man who stood there was *not* her Uncle Amos.

"I'm sorry," she said, as she turned to Jeremy. "I thought . . . you see, our mother died . . . Susannah's and mine. . . . Uncle Amos came and took everything we own. He and Aunt Cora . . ." She stopped, realizing that she was babbling. Mr. Caulfield would think she was foolish.

She heard the cry of "All aboard," and in a few minutes the car lurched as the train began to creep forward.

For the first time Sarah began to relax. She was actually on the way to Father. The wheels of the train set up a rhythm, a click and clack that went faster and faster and faster as the train swayed and rocked. *I'm on my way. On my way, my way, my way, my way.*

"I suppose I should explain," Sarah told Jeremy.

"Only if you wish," he said. "You can remain a woman of mystery if you'd rather. I make only one request."

"What's that?"

"That you tell me your name."

"Sarah Ann Lindley," she answered.

"Sarah Ann Lindley. Sarah," he said slowly, as though he were tasting the words, finding them delicious.

"You see, my uncle . . ." Sarah began, but Jeremy interrupted.

"Don't tell me, Miss Lindley. I can guess. You're a wealthy heiress escaping a cruel guardian who's trying to force you into a loveless marriage with one of those swells from the East Coast."

He grinned, but Sarah became serious. "You're partly right."

"I am?" She could see the heightened interest in his eyes.

"I'm not wealthy, and there's no loveless marriage involved," she said, "but Uncle Amos *is* a cruel guardian." She went on to explain about Susannah and her plan.

"Proper revenge," Jeremy said.

"Oh, no, Mr. Caulfield!" Sarah was shocked. "It's not revenge I'm after. It's simple justice."

"Of course, Miss Lindley," Jeremy said with a nod of apology, but there was that mischievous twinkle in his eyes again. "I should not have made such a wrong assumption. It's plain that you have a more noble spirit than I have."

Sarah was saved from trying to answer when Jeremy asked, "Just where is your father residing?"

"He's a miner—we think—in the town of Leadville, Colorado."

"Leadville!" In his excitement Jeremy grasped both of Sarah's hands, and she allowed him to hold them in spite of a shocked look from the plump woman who sat across the aisle. "It's fate!" he said. "I knew our meetings were not coincidence. They were designed to happen! I'm traveling to Leadville, too!"

Sarah couldn't help feeling suspicious. Maybe Jeremy Caulfield really was following her. She chose her next words carefully. "Just when did you decide that Leadville would be your destination?"

"I didn't," Jeremy said. "It was decided for me. My Uncle Chester owns a newspaper in Leadville, *The Daily Star,* and my father made up his mind that an apprenticeship on the newspaper would make a man of me—as he put it—and the hard work would drive nonsensical ideas out of my head."

Sarah was intrigued. "What kind of nonsensical ideas?"

"You might laugh if I tell you."

"I won't laugh." She held her right hand over her heart. "Promise."

"All right." Jeremy tucked his chin against his chest, stretched out his legs, and studied his shoes. "I want to be a published writer. Perhaps I'll write in a light vein like Mark Twain, or maybe compose something more serious in the style of Henry James. Maybe I'll write a travel piece like Jules Verne. Leadville will be just a temporary stop in my life. There's an exciting world out there to explore."

He paused, and Sarah said, "I think you have a wonderful goal. To be a published writer—that's impressive."

Jeremy looked up, obviously pleased at Sarah's reaction.

"You must love to read," Sarah said eagerly. "I do, too—especially the poets like Byron and Keats. Because I love to write poetry, too."

"I've never written a poem," Jeremy told her, "but if I did, it would be about a young woman with flyaway curls and golden eyes."

"Oh!" Sarah said. She pulled her hands away and immediately began tucking stray wisps of hair under her bonnet.

"I wish you'd take your bonnet off," Jeremy complained. "I'd like to watch the sunlight on your hair."

Sarah didn't answer. As she settled into place, smoothing her skirts and folding her hands in her lap while balancing herself against the sway of the railway car, Jeremy asked, "Are you always so prim and proper, Miss Lindley?"

"No," Sarah admitted. "That's the trouble. I'm usually impractical. But I have an important task to do, and I can't let anything get in the way."

"Anything? Or do you mean anyone?"

Sarah closed her eyes as heat rushed to her face. Why did she have to blush so easily? Susannah was right in saying that Sarah's face gave away whatever she was feeling.

Jeremy leaned a little closer and solemnly said, "If you're concerned about what I may think, I really have no objections to your being a little fuzzy-minded."

Sarah couldn't help what the woman across the aisle might think about correct public behavior. She tossed back her head and laughed.

The engine chugged south across Illinois and over the Mississippi River into St. Louis, Missouri. Sarah awoke as the train slowed with creaks and groans and an occasional shudder. She knew from the dingy streak of gray light that edged the windows that it must be very early in the morning.

They'd traveled most of the night, with only a few jarring stops and starts to shake the passengers from sleep. Around ten P.M. the porter had strolled through the car, dimming the gas lamps that hung at both the front and back; Sarah, in exhaustion and aching with loneliness for her sister, had rested her head against the hard window frame, her bonnet serving as a partial cushion as she fell asleep.

Sarah struggled to sit up. Where was her bonnet now? It dawned on her that it wasn't the window frame on which her head had been resting when she awoke. It was Jeremy Caulfield's shoulder! And his arm had been around her!

Sarah Ann Lindley, she scolded herself, *how could you be so bold? Sleeping on a man's shoulder without any thought of what is right and proper? What in the world does Mr. Caulfield think of such scandalous behavior?*

Fearfully, her face hot and stinging with embarrassment, Sarah dared to peek at Jeremy Caulfield from the corner of her eye. His head was back against the cushion, his eyes were tightly closed, and the arm nearest Sarah was outstretched on the seat where it had fallen when she sat up. Thankful that he was still asleep, Sarah quietly scooted to one side and stood. As she smoothed down her dress, she discovered her hat lying on the floor and attempted to brush and poke and bend it back to its proper shape. The way she was treating it, the poor thing would never last until she arrived in Leadville.

Others on the car were stirring now, and Sarah hurried toward the end of the car, to the small water closet in which she could freshen her appearance. She poured some water on one of the tiny linen towels piled on the cabinet and used it to wipe a few smudges of soot from her face and neck. She could not let out her hair and brush it in the cramped space, so Sarah had to content herself with brushing only the curls around her face and tucking in the wisps of hair that had escaped from the coil in back. When each hairpin had been tested and more firmly anchored, Sarah put on her bonnet, puffed out the bow under her chin, and went back to her seat in the railway car.

Jeremy was sitting up, stretching, and yawning, and he'd opened the curtains at the window. The train was creeping now, and Sarah could see city streets with houses and buildings.

"Good morning, Miss Lindley," Jeremy said.

"Good morning, Mr. Caulfield."

"Did you sleep well?"

She studied his eyes for any telltale signs of teasing, and there were none, but she cautiously said, "Very well, thank you."

"Good," he said. "I myself slept so hard, I can't remember the trip at all."

Sarah choked down a sigh of relief, quickly asking, "Where are we now?"

"St. Louis," Jeremy said. "Here's where we can get a filling breakfast before we change to the Missouri Pacific line, which will take us to Kansas."

Sarah realized how hungry she was. Yesterday evening Jeremy had shared with her the packet of bread and cheese and late fall pears which he'd brought with him. It hadn't occurred to her to bring food, and she felt inexperienced and foolish until she realized that it hadn't occurred to Susannah either.

Sarah sat next to Jeremy and braced herself as the train came to a jarring stop. She reached down to collect her carpetbag, but Jeremy had reached down, too, his fingers curling over hers. "Allow me, please, Miss Lindley," he said.

There was time for a large breakfast at a restaurant near the station, but the eggs were greasy, the potatoes limp, the ham tough, and the biscuits dry. Sarah was amazed. This was the first time she had eaten in a restaurant, and not only was she horrified at the inflated prices—Imagine! Fifty cents, which she'd insisted on paying herself—but she discovered that she was a much better cook than whoever had been paid to prepare these meals.

A red-faced gentlemen in a plaid suit sat at the next table. "Fred Harvey should come to St. Louis with his restaurants," he complained. "Those Harvey Houses along the route of the Atchison, Topeka, and Santa Fe know how to turn out a good meal—a thousand times better than this mishmash."

Anything would have been better, Sarah thought, but

she remembered that Jeremy had brought food on board yesterday, and she asked, "Should we get something to take on the train for our noon meal?"

Jeremy shook his head, and his eyes sparkled again. "Not this time," he said. "I've got a surprise for you."

Sarah smiled. Surprises were fun. Jeremy was fun. She was trying to be sensible and practical, but she couldn't be *all* the time.

Before she and Jeremy found places in one of the Missouri Pacific coach cars, Sarah had the opportunity to wash her face and neck again—this time with warm water and soap—and she brushed out her hair and coiled it back into place. Feeling much better, she joined Jeremy and climbed the steps of the nearest car.

As the train took off, Jeremy leaned back against the stiff, plush-upholstered seat and said, "It's going to be a long while—at least seven hours—before we reach Kansas City. Then even longer as we cross the state of Kansas. I'm thankful for such pleasant company on such a dangerous journey."

"Dangerous?" Sarah was surprised. "What do you mean by that?" She lowered her voice. "Indian attacks?"

"It's always a possibility. However, I'm here to protect you." He moved a little closer, and Sarah was grateful.

An elderly gentleman who sat in the seat in front of them turned around and frowned sternly at Jeremy. "I don't know where you are getting your information, young man, but it's faulty. There hasn't been an Indian attack on this line for a good many years."

"That's reassuring, sir," Jeremy said smoothly. "However, in speaking of danger I was mostly concerned about outlaws."

"Outlaws?" Sarah cried. "Oh, no! I told Susannah there might be outlaws!"

"Humph!" the man grunted as he turned back to face the front of the car. "I suppose we have to take our chances with those rapscallions as well as anyone else, but don't borrow trouble."

Sarah moved a little closer to Jeremy. "I've read about the outlaws in this area of the country," she said.

"We've all read about them," Jeremy told her as he took her hand in his. "The James brothers and the Younger brothers."

A man seated across the aisle leaned closer. "Don't forget Harley Emmett. He's caused a lot of trouble lately."

Some of the nearby passengers had overheard the conversation and nervously began discussing the wild Missouri boys who'd learned their sneak-attack warfare techniques in the Confederate army during the Civil War and were now using them to rob innocent people.

"I almost didn't come on this run," a man said to his companion, his voice booming through their section of the car, "when I heard that the James boys were hell-bent on getting revenge for the railway's agents testifying against them. Anybody traveling through Missouri during the next few months is taking his chances."

A woman gave a little shriek, and the babble of voices grew more excited.

For a moment Jeremy looked as worried as Sarah felt, but he lowered his voice so that only Sarah could hear. "Don't be afraid, Miss Lindley. I'll protect you."

There was something about the way he was looking at her. It began to dawn on Sarah that Jeremy may well have begun this conversation about outlaws in order to frighten her a little and make her feel more dependent upon him. That was a clever trick, but he wasn't going to get away with it.

"I think we should do as the gentleman seated in front of us suggested and not borrow trouble," Sarah told him. "I can't see any point in spending time worrying about a stupid band of outlaws."

Chapter 4

• • •

Sarah turned back toward the window, but in spite of her advice to Jeremy, she recalled some of the things she'd heard about outlaws.

Apparently all the outlaws operated in much the same way. When a train was being held up, they'd go from car to car robbing the passengers of their valuables. They'd take whatever money the men were carrying, and the women would often be instructed to remove their jewels and drop them into a hat or bag, along with the cash in their purses. Sarah owned no jewelry, and— she placed a reassuring hand to her midriff—the packet tucked into her corset should be safe. But what about the money in the reticule? She needed that for the stagecoach fare and the food she'd eat until she arrived in Leadville.

Trying to be unobtrusive, Sarah quietly opened the drawstrings on her purse, reached in, and pulled out the greenbacks, palming them so that they couldn't be seen.

"What are you doing?" Jeremy asked.

"Shhh!" Sarah said. She leaned close to him and whispered, "If we're robbed, those outlaws aren't going to get my money."

"How are you going to prevent that from happening?"

Sarah glanced around, positive that no one but Jeremy was watching, and slid her right hand behind her back. Poking and prodding, she managed to slip the thin fold of greenbacks into the crack between the seat and the padded back. She shifted position and glanced down. Good! The thick plush upholstery covered any telltale mark.

"Did you put all your money in there?" Jeremy asked.

"No. I left the coins and two silver dollars in my purse."

Jeremy thought a moment. "They may be wise to that trick."

"That's something we'll just have to find out," Sarah said, but she began to relax. It was a good, practical idea, and she was proud of it.

The landscape through which they passed was green and peaceful, with soft rolling hills. At times she glimpsed the Missouri River to the north. They came close enough, at one point, so that she waved through the open window at some children on the upper deck of a paddleboat, and they waved back.

Jeremy and Sarah talked of many things. They compared their childhoods and their dreams. While Jeremy spoke again of being a published writer, Sarah was surprised to discover that she had never given much thought to her future. *Why haven't I?* she wondered. *What is it I want?*

At the moment she had no answers, but when Jeremy

led the topic of conversation to Renoir, Monet, and the other French Impressionist painters and then on to the British-Zulu war, Sarah held her own.

She could tell that Jeremy had hoped to show off his knowledge and sophistication and was somewhat taken aback when she eagerly added to the conversation. Jeremy studied her for a moment and said, "I wouldn't think such a pretty girl would know so much about what is taking place in the world."

"Why not?" Sarah asked. "I told you that I love to read. I read the daily newspaper, too."

Jeremy smiled. "You become more and more fascinating by the moment, Miss Lindley."

Sarah smiled and glanced down modestly, but at that moment her empty stomach rumbled loudly.

Although she nearly died from embarrassment, Jeremy seemed not to have heard. He jumped to his feet and held out a hand to her. "It's time for the surprise," he said. "Come with me. There's a dining car on this train."

"We'll eat on the train?"

"Yes. The car's set with tables and chairs and white linen tablecloths."

Astounded, Sarah got to her feet and allowed Jeremy to take her elbow and steer her through the rocking cars to the dining car, where they were seated across from each other at one of the tables. The steward placed menus in their hands, and Sarah gasped in amazement. She had expected something simple, but the items on this menu were pure elegance, from the soup and fish dishes listed, through the roasts, wild game, and chicken croquettes, down to the coconut pudding, squash pie, assorted cakes, and cheeses.

"It's a feast!" Sarah exclaimed, but then she looked at the last statement on the menu: All Meals One Dollar. She hadn't guessed that travel could be so expensive. The waiter had placed a small plate of rolls on their table, and Sarah eyed them hungrily.

"Perhaps," she said to Jeremy, smiling a little as though the whole episode were amusing, "I might just have a roll or two, and a cup of tea." Suddenly a terrible thought occurred to her, and she dropped her pose to lean forward and whisper, "Or would that cost one dollar, too?"

"My dear Miss Lindley," Jeremy said, "I promised you a surprise. I am paying for your meal, and I'll be offended if you reject my gift."

Sarah blushed. "Mr. Caulfield, you know the proprieties. Please understand that I can't allow you to pay for my meal."

"Oh, hang the proprieties!" Jeremy answered. He ignored Sarah's openmouthed amazement and said, "You're not in a sheltered home in a civilized city. Your circumstances have changed drastically, and you'll have to change with them. Things are done differently in the West. For one thing, westerners have no use for all the ridiculous formality and pretense of what easterners suppose to be good manners."

As he leaned closer, his knee brushed against Sarah's, and—though she quickly moved away—she liked the sensation. Hoping Jeremy couldn't read her thoughts in her eyes, she challenged, "How do you know all this? You've never been West."

"I've learned about the West from my uncle's letters,"

he said. "And, Miss Lindley, I insist. I am paying for your meal."

Sarah's back stiffened. "Mr. Caulfield, the decision is not yours. It's mine and only mine."

Jeremy sighed and laid his menu on the table. Sarah could see the disappointment in his eyes. "Very well," he said. "You're a strong-minded woman."

Sarah? A strong-minded woman? Before she could argue, Sarah's stomach gave another rumble, this time inaudible, she hoped, and she smiled. "Thank you, Mr. Caulfield," she said. "My decision is to accept your generous offer. I'll have the tomato puree, the roast duck with currant jelly, and the assorted vegetables . . . to begin."

He grinned. "Fine. That's a good start. And may I drop this Miss Lindley business and call you Sarah? And will you call me Jeremy?"

Sarah already felt her behavior had been so bold that if Susannah knew, she'd be scandalized. But Susannah *didn't* know. Sarah had promised herself to take each day one step at a time, and she had just taken a major step. The power of thinking for herself and making her own decisions was exciting, and she was going to enjoy it wholeheartedly. "Not yet, Mr. Caulfield," she said, and handed him her menu.

Later, after they had returned to their coach, Sarah dozed—this time against the back of the seat. During her nap she felt Jeremy rest his head on her shoulder and, under the folds of her full skirt, his fingers gently intertwined with her own. His hand was warm and comforting, and without hesitation Sarah's fingers curled against his. She knew this was shocking public behavior, but for the moment she didn't care. What was it Jeremy had said about different circumstances and the way things were done in the West? Peacefully, contentedly, Sarah slumbered on.

The sun was a hot gold disk in the late afternoon when Sarah awoke. She reached to release the window curtain in order to cut the brilliant glare from her eyes and saw two horsemen riding toward the train. As they rode closer, she realized there was something odd about the appearance of the men.

"Jeremy!" she cried, reaching over to shake him awake. "There are men out there with bandannas over their faces!"

A moment later the train stopped with such a screech of brakes that packages tumbled into the aisles, and Sarah, who was perched on the edge of the seat, fell over, pulling Jeremy down with her.

Sprawled on top of Sarah, practically nose to nose with her, Jeremy struggled from sleep. "What happened?" he mumbled. "Train wreck? Are you hurt?"

Passengers shouted, a woman screamed, somewhere a child began to wail.

"Jeremy!" Sarah cried. "Help me up! The train's being robbed!"

Chapter 5

• • •

Jeremy and Sarah had no sooner scrambled to their feet than the door of their coach slammed open and a masked gunman, pushing a frightened conductor ahead of him, strode into the car. "Sit down!" he ordered, and everyone hurried to obey.

Sarah couldn't help staring at the outlaw. His shaggy dark hair and bandanna were grimy, and his heavy cotton shirt and pants were covered with dust. A broad-brimmed felt hat was pulled down so low on his head that it seemed to rest on his heavy eyebrows. He brandished a large handgun and ordered, "Don't anyone here try bein' brave, or they'll be buryin' you in the cemetery nearby in Independence."

There was the sound of many riders and orders being shouted. A rider reined in his horse just outside the car in which Sarah was sitting and thrust the end of his rifle into one of the open windows.

A woman gave a strangled shriek, but the outlaw in the coach ignored her. "Get out your valuables," he said. "Pocket watches, jewelry, and all your money. Drop them in here." He held out a bag and began to walk down the aisle among the passengers.

Sarah's heart pounded so loudly, she knew the gunman would be able to hear it. Her hands shook as he neared, and she closed her eyes as she held out her purse. But her eyes opened with a snap as the bag was roughly jerked from her hands.

"What's this?" As the gunman dumped the contents of Sarah's purse on the floor, her hairbrush and comb fell with a thud, and her train ticket and lace-trimmed handkerchief fluttered to one side. Sarah's few small coins and the two silver dollars rolled against his boot. "Where's your money?" he demanded.

"That's it," Sarah said in a tiny voice.

"That's all the traveling money you got with you?"

"Yes." She tried to look him straight in the eyes, but her glance slid away.

The man on horseback guffawed. "Look behind the seat," he called to the outlaw inside the coach. "That's where they always try to hide it."

Sarah was pulled roughly to her feet and shoved into the aisle. Jeremy stood, too, one arm around Sarah's shoulders to steady her as the gunman stepped past her and ran his fingers in the crack between the seat and the back rest. He came up with Sarah's small fold of greenbacks, studied them for a moment, then waved them under her nose. "You expect me to believe this is all the money you got?"

The man was unbearably rude, and to make things worse, he stank of sweat and dirt. But Sarah was so terrified of losing her money that she forgot to be afraid.

"Do you expect me to apologize because there's not more?" she snapped. Without giving him time to answer, she said, "That money is just enough to pay my stagecoach fare to Leadville and feed me until I arrive there to join my father. *I* need that money more than you do."

She actually reached out for the greenbacks, but the outlaw snatched them away. "Oh, ho!" he taunted. "Where'd you learn to act so hoity-toity? From your father? Who is he? A mayor? A wealthy businessman? Maybe he's the judge who put some of my boys in prison. Is he?"

The muscles around his eyes tightened as he grinned behind the bandanna, and that made Sarah even more angry. Jeremy put a restraining hand on her arm to warn her, but she shook it off. "Stop trying to frighten me," she told the gunman. "My father is a good man who works hard to get his money honestly, and not as you do."

"Miss Lindley," Jeremy cautioned, and tried to pull her to one side.

"Lindley?" the outlaw asked. "Your father's name is Lindley, and you say he lives in Leadville, Colorado? That wouldn't be Ben Lindley, would it?"

Sarah was so startled, it was difficult to speak, but she managed to say, "Yes. That's his name. Do you know him?"

"I know him." He peered into her face. "And I see the resemblance." The outlaw touched the brim of his hat as if he were going to remove it but suddenly seemed to change his mind. "Sorry," he mumbled, and to Sarah's surprise he thrust the bills into her hand and

43

strode to the rear of the car, ignoring the passengers who hadn't yet been robbed.

As he reached the doorway, he tossed a silver dollar to the conductor and said, "Here, have a drink on Jesse James."

Jesse James!

The outlaw was no sooner down the steps and on his horse than the people in the coach began milling and shoving and babbling to each other.

"Was that really Jesse James?" someone cried.

"He said he was."

"Oh, my!" an elderly woman murmured. "The famous outlaw!"

"Jesse James is the worst of the lot," the man seated in front of Sarah growled. "He should be strung up!"

Jeremy grabbed Sarah's shoulders, and his voice was rough with concern. "What did you think you were doing? Jesse James could have killed you!"

"Stop shaking me, Jeremy," Sarah demanded. "He didn't." As she pulled away, she waved the bills in front of Jeremy's nose. "And see—he let me keep my money."

She stooped to retrieve the contents of her purse, and Jeremy dropped to the floor beside her to help. "What you did was foolhardy," he insisted.

Sarah got to her feet, brushed off her skirt, and straightened her hat. She hung the cords of her purse over her left arm and drew herself up indignantly. "Ever since we met, you have taken it upon yourself to comment on my behavior, and now not a word of thanks to me that *you* weren't robbed," she began, but Jeremy interrupted.

"I just realized—you've been calling me Jeremy."

"I suppose I have."

His smile was almost as bright as the late afternoon glow in the wide, cloudless sky, and Sarah couldn't keep from smiling back.

"Thank you, Sarah," he said, and she continued to smile at him, liking the sound of her name on his lips.

The conductor bustled through the car, elbowing Sarah and Jeremy aside. "Back to your seats, ladies and gents. Everybody sit down," he ordered. "They've cleared the logs and brush from the tracks, and we'll be starting up in a few minutes. We aren't too far from Kansas City, but we've got to try to make up the time."

Sarah scooted close to Jeremy, hanging on to his arm while the train bucked and jolted as it started up again. "That outlaw knew my father," she told him.

Jeremy nodded.

"And he said 'sorry' to me. What did that mean?"

"Sorry that he had taken your money, I guess."

Sarah shook her head. "No. The way he said 'sorry' was different, as though he were saying it about my father."

"I'm sure he wasn't—"

"And he almost took off his hat. You saw that, didn't you?"

"What has that got to do with—?"

"As a mark of respect. As he'd do for someone who'd . . . who'd . . ." Sarah took a deep breath and murmured, "For someone who'd died."

Jeremy twisted to look into Sarah's eyes. "Don't start imagining things," he told her. "Jesse James said, 'I know him.' He didn't say he *knew* your father. That's what he would have said if your father had died."

Sarah sagged with relief against the seat back. "I think you're right," she said.

"Of course I'm right," Jeremy answered.

Sarah couldn't get her mind away from Jesse James. "Why would Jesse James know my father?" she asked.

"Maybe he's a person of importance in Leadville," Jeremy suggested.

"I doubt if a miner could have much importance."

"Are you sure he's a miner?"

"Well . . . no," Sarah admitted with surprise. "I assumed that because he'd gone to Leadville, his work would have to do with the mines there."

"Then your mother didn't tell you that your father is a miner?"

"No." Sarah was amazed how little about her family's life and her own life she had questioned.

"Maybe your father is like that Horace Tabor fellow who found a huge vein of silver," Jeremy said. "Maybe you'll find that he's very rich."

"Maybe," Sarah said, not wanting to discuss this any longer. If her father was wealthy or some important personage, Jesse James wouldn't have given back her money, would he? He would have been more inclined to take it. And if her father had become a lawman in the territory, James might have been very unfriendly.

But what if her father was also on the wrong side of the law?

That can't be! she said to herself, but her thoughts were interrupted as the train began jerking and creaking as it slowed to pass between small wooden shacks and false-front buildings.

"Kansas City," Jeremy announced. "Here's where we change trains again."

As they climbed on board one of the coach cars on the Kansas Pacific Railroad, Sarah and Jeremy discovered that railroad officials had stationed armed guards on the train.

"Are they expecting trouble?" Jeremy asked the conductor.

The man shook his head. "Nope. They're aimin' to avoid it."

A gentleman who was standing nearby hefted his satchel onto an overhead rack and said, "The Younger brothers have been spotted in these parts, and I heard there's been some trouble in Abilene."

Sarah was glad to see the tall, heavily armed man who had positioned himself at the front of their car. "Will the guards go with us as far as Abilene?" she asked.

"They'll go all the way to Denver," the conductor said. "Just three months ago there was trouble between the Santa Fe and the Denver and Rio Grande Railroad. The Kansas Pacific wants to stay out of it."

"What kind of trouble?" Jeremy asked.

"More'n one railroad wants the rights to build a route to Leadville," the conductor said. "The Santa Fe folks got hold of some hired guns under Bat Masterson and Doc Holliday, so the D and RG people put together their own army of about one hundred special deputies and the sheriff, and the two groups fought it out in a free-for-all."

47

"But these weren't common outlaws. They were big companies!" Sarah said. "Couldn't they just talk out their problems?"

"They did that eventually, after a bunch of their men got shot, and the D and RG got back its railroad."

"They shot at each other?"

"This is the West, Sarah," Jeremy said. "People out here aren't civilized, as they are in Chicago." He took her elbow and steered her to a seat, shoving their bags underneath.

Two men who had been passengers on the Missouri Pacific began to tell the conductor about the robbery they'd just experienced. Sarah paid them no attention and looked out the window to the railroad yard, wishing with all her heart she could quickly find her father and take him out of the West. What was Benjamin Lindley—who had once read his daughter poetry and sung ballads of love to her mother by firelight—doing in a wild place like Colorado where businessmen hired killers to shoot at each other?

Chapter 6

•   •   •

The ride across Kansas was uneventful as the train sped at forty miles an hour across the gradual rise of the seemingly flat land. The tall silvered prairie grasses and the patches of shimmering wheat nearly ripe for harvest rippled toward the horizon like the waves on Lake Michigan when the wind shivered across its surface.

Sarah slept and ate, this time insisting on paying for her own meal. As she talked for endless hours with Jeremy, she began to understand the loneliness of this young man. Jeremy's eyes were so much like her father's that Sarah began to wonder in what other ways the two men might be alike. Had Father also been lonely?

It occurred to Sarah that soon she'd be saying good-bye to Jeremy and returning with Father to Chicago. Her throat tightened, and she fastened her gaze upon Jeremy's deep brown eyes, attentive to every word he had to say.

By the time the train slowed for its approach to Denver, Sarah felt grimy and sticky. Oh, how she wanted a bath! But as they left the prairie heat behind and climbed to a higher altitude, it had grown gradually cooler, just as Susannah had known it would.

When the train stopped, Sarah rested her carpetbag on the seat and opened it, finding her blue wool coat neatly folded at the top. Sarah gratefully tugged it out of the bag and tried to shake out the wrinkles; as she did, she heard the plop of something falling to the floor.

Jeremy bent and picked up a very small package wrapped in paper. "This fell from your bag," he said.

Slowly Sarah unwrapped the package, unwinding it from fold after fold of the stiff paper, until the object within lay in the palm of her hand.

"It's a pin," Jeremy said as he leaned over Sarah's shoulder to see what she had found. "Garnets and silver. Very pretty."

The pin blurred into streaks of deep red and glittering light as Sarah felt the dampness on her cheeks. All the exhaustion, the fears, and the loneliness for both her mother and Susannah rushed to escape through her tears, and Sarah did nothing to stop them.

"Oh, Sarah! Don't cry," Jeremy said, distress in his voice, but as Sarah continued to weep, he held her tenderly and silently and allowed her to cry against his shoulder.

Finally Sarah stepped back, wiped her eyes with the almost-clean linen handkerchief Jeremy handed to her, and carefully pinned the band of garnets and silver across the neck of her blouse.

Jeremy studied her and shook his head. "They want us off the train as soon as possible, but can you find time to wash your face? The tears and the soot weren't a very good mixture."

Sarah laughed, thankful that Jeremy had the power to lift her spirits, and hurred to the tiny water closet to mop her face and neck with the small amount of cold water left in the pitcher.

Inside the depot Sarah and Jeremy discovered that the next stage to Leadville would not leave until the following morning at nine. Carrying their bags, they walked the short distance from the railroad station to the Denver office of Spotswood and McClelland's and purchased their tickets.

Twenty-three dollars for the fare! Sarah watched the amount of cash in her purse shrink to very little. *Never you mind,* she told herself, trying to calm her anxieties. *The packet of money that traveled next to my skin all the way to Colorado will be enough to bring Father and me back to Chicago. Susannah said so.*

After she and Jeremy stepped back out of the office and onto the wooden sidewalk, Sarah hesitated. "What now?" she asked. "The stage won't leave until tomorrow morning."

"In the meantime, tell me your greatest wish. What would you like best in the whole world right this very minute?" Jeremy asked.

Sarah sighed dreamily and without a second thought said, "Oh, if wishes could only come true! I wish I could have a bath. And a real bed to sleep in."

As Jeremy smiled, Sarah blushed furiously. What had she said? She couldn't believe that she had actually spoken to a male acquaintance about two very intimate things! And there was no way to undo the damage.

Embarrassed, Sarah turned so that Jeremy couldn't see her face.

But he gently took her shoulders and turned her around. "Spoken like a true westerner," he said. "As I told you, circumstances are different here, and so are archaic rules for manners. In my uncle's last letter he recommended a well-established Denver hotel to me, and I think we'll find it at the end of this block."

Sarah hadn't planned on an overnight stay in a hotel. She had never even set foot in a hotel. She had assumed all along that she'd leave one carrier to climb into another.

But she had trusted Jeremy this far, so with Jeremy carrying his bag in one hand and Sarah's in the other, the two of them picked their way down the uneven wooden sidewalk until they came to the front door of the hotel. It was a large brick structure, with roof turrets on the fourth floor and gargoyles framing the doorways and windows of the main floor.

As they stepped inside the lobby, Sarah drew a sharp breath of appreciation. What a beautiful, elegant room!

The floors and lower portions of each wall were paneled in a dark, highly polished wood. The upper walls sported an ornate, dark red wallpaper, over which hung countless paintings. Oriental rugs, heavily carved tables, and plush-covered sofas with curved arms and claw feet were scattered around the room. Deep red velvet drapes edged each window, and gold silk tassels and fringe hung thickly over the padded cornices, the tables, and even some of the chairs.

"This way," Jeremy said, and Sarah followed him to a highly polished desk, where he spoke to a clerk.

As Jeremy put down the bags, a boy jumped to pick them up. The clerk glanced at Sarah, nodded respectfully to Jeremy, and handed him a pen.

In turn Jeremy gave the pen to Sarah. "Write your name and home address," he said, and moved out of the way so that she could reach the large guest book with its creamy white paper.

Jeremy and Sarah followed the boy with their bags toward the stairs and climbed to the third floor. Outside one of the rooms, the boy stopped, opened the door with a flourish, and held it wide. "This is your room, miss," he said.

It was a corner room, light and airy, with a breeze ruffling the sheer curtains at one of the windows.

The boy put Sarah's carpetbag on a low, square table, handed her a door key, and trotted out into the hall to join Jeremy. "This way, sir," he said, but Jeremy took a step toward Sarah.

"After your bath, get some rest," he said. "We have a reservation for dinner at seven."

For the first time Sarah had misgivings. "Isn't all this terribly expensive?" she whispered.

"No," Jeremy said.

Sarah wanted an explanation, but she was aware of the boy's eyes on her. She ducked back into her room and locked the door.

"A bath! At last I'm going to have a bath!" she cried. She laid her coat across the foot of the bed, tossed her bonnet toward the table, and flung herself across the bed.

But she jumped to her feet at the sound of a loud knock. Sarah opened the door to admit four women wearing white starched aprons over their dark dresses, each woman carrying two buckets of steaming water. Behind them came a man who was bent over, carrying a round, enameled tub on his shoulders. The group marched into the room, put down the tub a few feet away from the foot of the bed, and poured water into it. From somewhere a painted wooden screen appeared. It was unfolded and set up to curve around the tub, and on it were hung two large towels, thicker and softer than any Sarah ever before had seen.

As the windows were closed, one of the women said, "There is soap on the stool by the tub, miss, and if you wish to wash your hair, I'll bring you a vinegar rinse."

"Oh, I'd like that," Sarah answered. "Thank you."

The parade marched out of the room, and Sarah shut the door. She waited impatiently, but the woman didn't return with the vinegar rinse.

Finally Sarah gave up. She pulled off her clothes, laid them on the bed with her money packet, and climbed into the tub. She slid down until the water reached her neck, humming to herself with pleasure.

When the knock at the door came, it startled her. "Oh!" she said, and reached for one of the large bath towels hanging on the screen. "One minute," she called.

But as she scrambled to her feet, trying to wrap herself in the towel without dropping the ends in the tub, she heard the door open and softly close. "Oh, dear!" she cried again. She realized she'd forgotten to lock the door, and was surprised that the woman would enter her room without permission.

"Leave the rinse by the door, please," Sarah began, and stretched to peer over the screen. But it wasn't the white-starched woman she saw. It was a thin, wiry boy, probably no older than ten or eleven, who turned from the bed to stare up at Sarah.

Sarah gasped and clutched the towel tightly. "What are you doing here?" she screeched.

The boy grinned. He took a step toward Sarah and waved his right hand. In it was Sarah's money packet.

Chapter 7

* * *

"You can't have that!" Sarah yelled at the boy.

Taunting her, he stepped up to the screen. "Who's gonna stop me? You, without no clothes on?"

"You wicked little urchin!" Sarah cried. Determined not to lose her money, she stepped onto the rim of the tub and stretched out an arm, lunging at him. To Sarah's surprise and the boy's, the screen toppled over with Sarah on top and the boy pinned underneath.

Sarah got to her knees, thankful that the tub hadn't gone over, too, and tried to reach the towel she'd been wearing, but it had flown to one side. The other towel was somewhere under the screen.

"Ooooooh," the boy cried, "get off! Get off! That's my stomach you're tramplin' on. You're killin' me!"

"That might be a good idea," Sarah snapped. Beneath her the screen shook as the boy tried to squirm free, but Sarah gave it a sound thump.

"Ouch! You got my head that time!" he complained.

"Good," Sarah said. "I'll do it again if you don't lie

still." Thank goodness he couldn't see through the screen, but if someone else should come into the room, they'd find her here without a stitch. The idea was so mortifying that Sarah closed her eyes and shuddered.

The boy gave a sudden lurch, but Sarah kept her balance and pounded the screen harder than she had before. "I told you to hold still," she demanded.

Sarah realized that if she moved a little bit closer to the bed, she could reach her coat. She inched forward, making sure she was firmly on top of the boy while he squawked, "My chest! You keep this up, and I'll be dead afore long!"

"Be quiet, you little thief!" Sarah, furious that she could have lost all her money, was unmoved. She managed to reach her coat and pull it on, and—once she was no longer exposed—felt more in control of the situation. She plopped herself down firmly on a spot where she imagined the boy's lower limbs might be, ignored his complaints, and said, "I suppose the best thing for me to do right now is to begin screaming. When someone comes to find out what's wrong, I can turn you over to them."

"Oh, please don't do that, miss," the boy said, and began loudly to sob and snuffle.

"Stop that," Sarah said.

He did as she ordered, but he pleaded, "They'll hang me, you know. I'm as good as dead if you turn me in."

"Don't be silly," Sarah told him. "They don't hang children."

"I'm thirteen. I'm old enough."

"If you know this might happen to you, then why are you a thief?"

His voice was muffled by both the screen and his tears. "I never been anythin' else."

"Do your parents know what you're doing?"

"Far as I know, I never had no parents."

Sarah gave a long sigh and tried to think. "The fact is that you tried to steal my money."

"Fact is, I ain't really stole it yet," he answered. "It just happens to be in my hand."

"Can you wiggle your hand out to the top of the screen?" Sarah asked. "The one with the money in it, I mean."

The body underneath her wiggled and squirmed, and the edge of the packet of money appeared above the screen. As Sarah grasped it, the boy asked, "Now will you let me up, miss?"

"As soon as I count it," Sarah said. She settled herself more comfortably, paying no attention to the grunts and groans coming from under the screen, and counted the money. "Some of it's missing," she said.

"Think o' that!" the boy said. "You been robbed before?"

"Give it to me," Sarah said, "before I say *three*." When he didn't answer, she began to count, "One . . . two . . ."

The screen heaved, and his other hand shot upward. Sarah leaned over to snatch the bills from his clenched fingers.

"Now will you let me up?" he begged.

Sarah folded the rest of the money inside the packet. Suppose she let him go. She had the advantage right now because she was sitting on him, but when he was free, there would be nothing to stop him from giving her a clout on the head, grabbing her packet, and running. "Not yet," she said. "I'll tell you when."

In less than two minutes, there was another knock at her door. "Come in!" Sarah called.

"You shouldn't leave your door unlocked, miss," the woman with the vinegar rinse began, but she broke off with a gasp as she saw Sarah. "What is it? Have you fallen? Are you hurt?"

"I'm fine," Sarah said, "though the screen may have suffered a scratch or two. There's a boy pinned underneath."

"Whatever for?" The woman's eyes were wide with shock.

"I should have had enough sense to lock my door after you left," Sarah told her. "This boy I'm sitting on let himself in my room and tried to steal my money, but I caught him in time."

"Let me up!" came a smothered cry. "There's no feelin' left in my legs!"

The woman dropped her deferential pose and began to laugh. "If it's the rapscallion I think it is, what you've done to him serves him right. I'll go downstairs and get some help."

"Wait," Sarah said. "He told me that if we turn him in, he'll be hanged."

The woman thought a minute. "And well he might be. He's snooped around and caused trouble here before."

Sarah began to soften. "He's just a boy."

"Born bad."

"No one's born bad," Sarah insisted. "He still has the opportunity to change his ways."

"I'll change 'em! I'm changin' right now," came the voice from under the screen.

"What do you want to do, miss?" the woman asked.

Sarah addressed the boy again. "If I get up, will you skedaddle out of this hotel and never come back?"

"Promise! And I'll never steal again!"

"What will you do to earn your living?"

With only a moment's hesitation, the woebegone voice cried, "I'll get me a job cleanin' out the horse stalls down at the stable."

The woman suppressed a smile as Sarah looked up.

"Do you think he means it?" Sarah asked.

"Not for a minute."

"Just give me a chance," the boy pleaded.

Sarah kept a firm grip on her packet of money as she crawled off the screen. She stood next to the woman and said to the boy, "All right. Now you may climb out."

As soon as he was on his feet, she ordered, "And put up the screen the way it had been."

When this was done to her satisfaction, Sarah tried to be stern as she said, "You may go, young man. Just remember your promises."

The boy ran to the door, paused as he opened it, and grinned with all the malice and mischief she might have expected before he disappeared into the hallway.

"Hopeless," Sarah said.

The woman nodded.

"But I didn't want him hanged."

They both sighed, and the woman said, "You'll still be wanting your bath, so we'll add a little more hot water to the tub." She glanced at the dusty skirt and blouse that Sarah had been wearing. "If you like, I'll brush your skirt and use a little Fullers Earth on that shirtwaist and have them back to you by this evening."

"Oh, thank you!" Sarah said, her good mood returning rapidly. "I'd be very grateful."

When more hot water had been brought and the door securely locked, Sarah placed her money packet next to the tub where she could keep a close eye on it. She pulled out the pins in her hair, letting it flow down her back, and sank blissfully under the warm, cleansing water. It had been at least a month since she'd had a bath in a tub. It was pure, wonderful luxury.

When the knock at the door came, and a voice called, "Six o'clock, miss," Sarah answered, but she wiggled and stretched and allowed herself to wake slowly. Her body was clean, her hair was clean, the bed was clean—and gloriously comfortable. She thought of the hours—the days—of soot and dust and prairie heat. *Why would anyone want to travel who didn't absolutely have to?*

Sarah sat up, suddenly hungry as she remembered her dinner appointment with Jeremy. She took some money from her packet and tucked it into the reticule.

Sarah was surprised to discover near the top of the carpetbag her pale peach dress of cotton lawn with the wide lace collar, which Susannah had tucked in among her serviceable traveling clothes. She laid the dress across the bed, smoothing out many of the wrinkles, and fastened the garnet and silver pin over the knot of lace at the V of her neckline.

By the time Jeremy knocked at her door, calling, "Sarah? Are you ready?" Sarah was dressed, her money packet tucked in place under her corset. Even after a half hour of constant brushing, her long mass of hair was still slightly damp; but she had swept it up, curling the short bangs and ringlets over her finger, and it gleamed like a dark red halo in the glow from the oil lamp on the table. She opened the door and saw Jeremy's eyes widen with appreciation.

"Oh, Sarah," he said, "you're even more beautiful than I remembered."

"Don't," Sarah said and put her hands to her cheeks.

With a teasing grin Jeremy took her hands and pulled them down. "The blush is becoming. Now get your purse and let's go to the dining room. Are you as hungry as I am?"

"Yes," Sarah answered, glad that the money packet had kept her from pulling her corset strings as tightly as she usually did.

There were no menus in the beautiful dining room with gilt chairs and molded, painted cherubs on the ceiling. The waiters simply brought their food, and after a first course of river trout, they were served slices from roasted antelope meat, covered with a dark wine-flavored gravy. On the plate were boiled small potatoes and a strange kind of yellow squash. The meal ended with pastries and coffee, and Sarah wished she had worn another dress with a little larger waistline.

When they had finished eating, Jeremy signaled to their waiter, and he came to pull out Sarah's chair. As Sarah reached for the purse on her lap, she whispered to Jeremy, "Whom do we pay?"

"Shhh," Jeremy said. "It's taken care of."

Sarah took his arm and walked beside him as they

left the dining room, but as soon as they were in the hotel lobby, she said, "What do you mean, it's taken care of?"

"It was paid for in advance."

"Then tell me what my share is, so that I can repay you."

"Sarah," Jeremy said, laughter in his eyes, "I invited you to dinner. That means that I must pay."

"That's hardly fair," Sarah began, but Jeremy interrupted.

"Haven't you ever gone out socially with a young man?"

"Why, no," Sarah answered. "I haven't."

"A beautiful girl like you? It's hard to believe that men weren't lined up, wanting to court you."

Embarrassed, Sarah fumbled for words. "There has always been the boardinghouse to care for. Besides, Mother thought eighteen was a suitable age for courtship, and I'm only seventeen."

"Seventeen is a perfect age for courtship." Jeremy tucked his other hand over Sarah's fingers and led her to one of the sofas at the side of the parlor.

"But Mother thought . . ." Sarah protested.

Jeremy interrupted as he seated himself beside her. "Your mother is no longer making decisions for you, Sarah. The direction your life takes now is up to you."

Sarah looked into his eyes and saw a spark she hadn't seen before. It wasn't mischief. Was Jeremy as serious as she suspected he might be? Was he hinting about marriage?

"Jeremy," she said, "my only plan right now is to find my father and bring him home to Chicago. I have no right to make any other decisions."

"I understand," he said, "but think beyond that. There is a good possibility that your father may travel home with you within a week or two. What next? You must have hopes beyond that."

Sarah hesitated. Forced to face her dreams, she realized they had been those of a child, spun of poetry and magic, with no more substance than a handful of old cobwebs.

"You told me," she said to Jeremy, "that Leadville would be just a temporary stop in your life, that there's an exciting world out there to explore."

Jeremy nodded, and Sarah continued. "Perhaps there's a world for me to explore, too, but my dreams haven't taken me there yet. I need more time, Jeremy."

"Then that's what you'll have," Jeremy answered tenderly. But before Sarah could answer, he abruptly changed the subject to Leadville, and Sarah could detect the growing excitement in his voice. "I spoke with some travelers in the hotel lobby this afternoon. Be prepared for a town that has gone wild, with gamblers and armed thieves and footpads. People are being robbed in the streets in broad daylight, and no one is safe outside after dark."

Oh, no! More of this horrible western lawlessness? Sarah wondered if she should tell Jeremy about the boy who had entered her room and tried to steal her money. No, the news would only upset him. Perhaps he'd even scold her for not turning the boy over to the authorities. Besides, how could she explain falling off the rim of the bathtub without a stitch on?

"I suppose it's best to be prepared," Sarah said. "If we have time, before the stagecoach leaves, I would like to buy an umbrella, one with a sturdy knob on the handle."

Jeremy chuckled. "An umbrella? In a town in which men are armed with knives and guns?"

Sarah pictured herself with a gun in her hands and shivered. "I could never shoot anyone, Jeremy," she said.

"But you *could* rap them on the head with your umbrella handle? Sarah! Where is your conscience?" When Jeremy finished laughing, he said, "Never mind. I'll be there to take care of you."

Sarah couldn't help smiling. Both on the train and here in the hotel, she had done a good job of taking care of herself; but as Jeremy went on to talk about the wealth being found every day in the silver carbonate mines of Leadville, Sarah thought ahead to the daylight robberies and the footpads at night. What was Father doing in a dangerous place like that? And again she wondered, why did the train robber know her father?

Chapter 8

•   •   •

Early the next morning Sarah dressed in her freshened traveling skirt and shirtwaist, repacked her bag, and breakfasted with Jeremy. When she attempted to pay her hotel bill, however, the clerk informed her that payment had already been made.

At that moment Jeremy stepped up beside Sarah and smilingly presented her with an umbrella—a sturdy black one with a heavy carved handle. "Just what you ordered," he said.

Sarah thanked him, but her mind was not on umbrellas at the moment. She drew him aside and said, "Even in the West I'm sure that it's not proper for a gentleman to pay a lady's traveling expenses. Since you've already paid the hotel clerk, then tell me the amount so that I can reimburse you."

Jeremy tried to protest. "Please let me help you, Sarah. I know this wasn't an expense you had planned on."

"That's right," Sarah said. "But it was I who made

the decision to stay here, and it's my decision, too, to pay my own way." Surprised and pleased at the firm direction she'd taken, Sarah tucked a hand inside her purse. "How much do I owe you, Jeremy?"

Jeremy thought a moment. "Three dollars," he said.

Three dollars would take a large bite out of her traveling money, but Sarah handed three one-dollar greenbacks to Jeremy, whose lips were set and serious, but whose eyes were laughing.

"Is something funny?" Sarah challenged as she pulled on her gloves.

"Of course not," Jeremy said. He pocketed the money, picked up her carpetbag and his own, and said, "We'd better hurry if we want to get seats on the stage."

A large new and gleaming Concord stagecoach was parked near the Spotswood and McClelland offices. The driver's seat was perched on high, in front of a rack to hold baggage, and an extra passenger seat on top faced the back. On the side doors of the stage were painted a replica of the nation's eagle, a red, white, and blue shield clutched in its claws, and over its head the words: U.S. MAIL. A four-horse team was already hitched in place.

While Jeremy handed their bags to a man who was tossing them up on top, where they were strapped down, Sarah walked toward the front of the coach to look at the horses.

"Aren't you beautiful," she crooned to the nearest horse, and reached out a gloved hand to pat the white patch on his nose.

To her surprise the horse raised his head, whinnying loudly. Sarah's wrist was gripped, and she was jerked backward, nearly losing her balance. A muscular, broad-shouldered man with a gun belt resting on his narrow hips shoved in front of her, grabbed the reins, and spoke soothingly and firmly to the lead horse until it quieted. Then he turned to Sarah, and she found herself looking into eyes as deep blue as a late afternoon sky. Their owner was young, too—maybe a year or two younger than Jeremy—and the hair that curled from under his wide-brimmed, stained felt hat was black and thick. He was one of the handsomest men Sarah had ever seen.

"Never come on to a horse suddenlike, the way you did," he said, "especially one that's hitched to a team."

Sarah was used to city voices that were clipped, some of them a little nasal; and from the time she'd arrived in the West, she'd heard voices that twanged like banjo strings off-key. But this man's voice was as softly slurred as butter warmed by the sun, and it took Sarah a moment to realize she'd been scolded.

"I—I didn't know. I'm s-sorry," she stammered.

"We'll be traveling together, ma'am. I just needed to get you used to the setup," he said. "We'll be ready to go soon as you and your husband get into the coach."

"My hus—?" Sarah stood as tall as she could, almost looking this man eye to eye, and said, "I do not have a husband. I am traveling alone."

His eyes widened. "Alone? To Leadville?"

Sarah could see him taking a good look, trying to estimate what kind of person she was and what she'd be doing in a place like Leadville, and to her amazement tears came to her eyes. She didn't care what this stranger thought. It was no one's business but her own. She turned abruptly and marched back to the stage.

Most of the passengers had boarded, many of the men choosing to sit on top. Sarah climbed inside the coach and sat next to two women with powdered and rouged faces. Since they'd all be seat companions, Sarah turned to smile pleasantly, but they ignored her. It was just as well. Sarah could see a dingy neck and a grubby streak of dirt around the hairline of the woman next to her, and in spite of a sickening-sweet perfume, the woman smelled like scrub rags on a damp, humid day.

Sarah leaned on the frame of the open coach window and smiled across the aisle at Jeremy, who was wedged in between two portly gentlemen, one wearing a heavy wool suit and a broad-brimmed hat, the other dressed in a dark plaid overcoat and a deerstalker hat with the flaps down over his ears. Sarah's bonnet, gloves, and coat were comfortable in the chill morning air, but the gentlemen seemed prepared for real cold. Leadville was in high mountain country, and Sarah hoped that they didn't know something about the climate which she should have known, too.

She heard someone call, "Ready to go, Clint," and she saw the dark-haired man swing himself up to the driver's seat. So . . . his name was Clint. A sharp, dark name like the steel blade of a knife or the hard stone that sharpened it, sending off sparks as the metal struck. Clint . . . flint . . . Clint.

As the stage rumbled and shook along the rough road going southwest, Sarah hung on tightly. They were making good time, and once out of Denver, she watched the landscape change as they climbed higher. Pines and blue spruce grew thicker and taller; and aspen, their leaves turning in the chill of late summer, were splatters of gold against the rocky hillsides.

Jeremy introduced himself to the two men, and Sarah heard the one in the deerstalker cap curtly tell him that his name was George H. Fryer.

"Fryer Hill! It's named for you!" Jeremy seemed excited, and the talk turned to Fryer's success with the *New Discovery Mine.*

This meant nothing to Sarah, and she was equally uninterested in the second man, who was more affable, but still pompous as he made sure that they'd all remember Homer Morton, the most prosperous and influential banker in Leadville.

Jeremy then smiled at Sarah, introducing her to his two seat companions.

Homer Morton squinted at Sarah. There was a puzzled look in his eyes as though he should know her but couldn't quite remember when or where they'd met. "Could it be that you're a schoolteacher?" he asked. "I heard that one of the young ladies who has the job is engaged to be married and wants to be replaced."

"I'm not a teacher," Sarah said. "In fact, I'm not going to stay in Leadville. I've come only to find my father, Benjamin Lindley. Perhaps you know him?"

Mr. Fryer continued to look dour, but Sarah saw a flash of recognition in Mr. Morton's eyes. She leaned forward eagerly, trying to maintain her balance as she waited for what he might tell her; but his expression changed, and he said, "Sorry, Miss Lindley. I don't believe that name's ever come to my attention."

He's lying to me, Sarah thought. She was shocked and

a little frightened. *He knows my father. I could see it in his face. Why should he lie about it?*

As she sank back against the cushioned seat, she became aware that the woman with the dirty neck was looking at her with a wary expression of distrust. *She knows my father, too,* Sarah thought, but of course she couldn't ask the woman about him. Not here. Not now. The other woman spoke to her companion, addressing her as Lily, and Lily turned away from Sarah.

Why should the people who know Father have such a strange reaction to his name?

Jeremy fell into a conversation with the banker, who began to discuss Leadville's Silver King, Horace Tabor, and the great good fortune he'd had with the *Matchless Mine;* but Sarah clutched her umbrella with her left hand, and the frame of the open window with her right, and rode silently, preferring to study the scenery and think about Father.

She was so close to seeing him again. Would she recognize him? Would he recognize her? What would she say to him? She couldn't just blurt out the news about Mother. Even though Father had left his wife and children, she knew he must still love them. *Oh, Father,* she silently cried. *Father, please come home with me to Chicago!*

The stage rolled to a stop, and the door next to her feet was thrown open. "Fifteen minutes' stop while we change horses. You've got time to stretch your legs," Clint announced to the passengers, but his eyes were on Sarah.

Clint held out a hand, so Sarah took it, bent to get through the doorway, and climbed down the steps placed next to the coach. Clint's hand was so large that hers almost disappeared in it. The skin was rough and callused, and she could feel the strength in his fingers. "Thank you," she murmured, not daring to look at his face for fear he'd be able to read her thoughts through her eyes.

They seemed to be at some kind of office set up near a deserted railway station. Sarah briskly strode around to the back of the station, where she found what she was looking for—a privy.

When she returned, Jeremy told her, "It's going to be rough from here on up to Leadville."

"Is it the weather?" Sarah asked. The sky was almost cloudless, but it was much cooler than it had been in Denver, and she thought of the men in their winter clothes.

"There should be no problem with severe weather," Jeremy assured her. "It's the road. It runs through Weston Pass, where the rock has been blasted away, but the surface is narrow and rocky with more than a few bad places in it, according to our driver."

Clint, Sarah thought. Again in her mind she could hear the clang of metal against flint in a shower of sparks.

As to the road—it had already been so rough, she couldn't imagine how it could get much worse and still be called a road. "I'm game for it," she said. "We really haven't got a choice, have we?"

Jeremy smiled and held out an elbow to Sarah. She was about to take his arm when Clint strode up and said to Jeremy, "That satchel of yours seems to have come undone. I'd thank you to climb up and make sure nothing's been lost out of it, then fasten it up again."

"How could the straps have come undone?" Jeremy began, but Clint interrupted.

"Who knows? Rough road, maybe." He stared at Jeremy until Jeremy gave in and hurried toward the stage, muttering under his breath.

Sarah took a step forward, too, but Clint moved into her path. He touched the brim of his hat and said, "The name's Clint Barnes, ma'am. I came up a mite short with you in the beginning, and I apologize for that. It wasn't a good way to begin a friendship."

His eyes were so blue! Sarah brought her mind back to what he had said and answered, "You don't have to apologize, Mr. Barnes. You did the right thing in cautioning me."

He smiled, and Sarah thought that the smile in his weather-browned face was like the sun touching the browned mountain ridges.

"We go by first names here in the West," he told her. "Some people, if they've got any last names, don't tell 'em." He paused and said, "I'd like it if you'd call me Clint."

Why not? Sarah thought. *Against everything I've ever been taught, I'm on a first-name basis with Jeremy.* She nodded.

"Thank you, ma'am," Clint said.

Sarah shook her head. "It doesn't sound right for me to call you Clint and you to call me ma'am."

He grinned. "If it pleases you, I'll call you Sarah."

"You know my name?"

"I've got the passenger list." His expression became serious. "I don't know what reason you've got for going to Leadville, but I think you're making a mistake.

73

Leadville's a rough town. It's not the place for a lady like you. We could put you up at a ranch near here, and you could catch the other stage back."

"I'm going to Leadville to find my father," Sarah told him. "My mother has died, and I need to inform my father and bring him home to take care of my younger sister and me."

"I'm sorry," Clint said. He rested his hand on her arm so gently that Sarah caught her breath. "What's your father's name? Maybe I can help you find him."

Sarah, conscious only of Clint's touch, struggled to pull her thoughts together. "Thank you," she said. "That's very kind of you. My father's name is Benjamin Lindley."

She waited for Clint's reaction, but he shook his head and said, "I never heard of him, but that don't mean anything, because I'm in and out of Leadville driving the stage."

"That must be an interesting job," she said politely, but Clint shook his head.

"It's a job straight out of—beggin' your pardon, Sarah—out of you-know-where. I grew up herding cows, so I'm working as a stagecoach driver only long enough to save the money I need to buy me the ranch I've got my heart set on."

"Oh," Sarah said. "You're a cowboy!"

"Cowhand. You make it sound exciting."

"Well, isn't it?"

"Nope. Being a cowhand means long hours with little sleep, and low wages, and bad food, and more dust and dirt in a month than anyone should swallow in a life-time. You're up against rustlers, sheepherders who're after your land, stampedes, and sometimes even mountain lions and wolves."

"Then why do you like the job?"

"Because there are good moments you wouldn't find anyplace else—working a night watch under stars big as your fist, singing soft to the cattle so they won't get spooked, feeling a good horse under you and knowing the two of you are a team, and that nothing's going to stop you from getting those cattle to market." He stopped and ducked his head almost shyly. "It'll be even better when those cattle are my own."

Jeremy joined them, his lips tight with annoyance. "The straps on my satchel were unbuckled, all right," he said. "I'd like to know how they got that way."

"No telling," Clint said easily. "Nothing was missing, was there?"

"Nothing was missing," Jeremy said. He glared at Clint, but Clint didn't seem to notice or care.

"Then let's get going," Clint said. Without another word to Sarah, he got his passengers back on the coach and climbed up on the seat, and the big Concord coach swung off on the mountain road toward Leadville.

Jeremy had been right. The road was bumpier than it had been before. At times a wheel dipped into a rut or a gully, and the coach rocked crazily. Twice Sarah held the back of one gloved hand against her mouth to keep from crying out.

"We're not going to tip over," Jeremy told her firmly.

"Don't be too sure," the woman who was called Annie Mae said to him. "Last time I made this trip, we went over three times."

"That's outrageous!" Jeremy said as he tried to keep his balance. "The company should hire a good driver."

"Clint's a good driver," she told him. "In fact, he's one of the best."

With that the coach gave a gigantic heave, and Sarah found herself flying through the air. Creaking and thudding, the coach toppled over.

Someone's elbow landed in Sarah's face, and a booted foot pushed against her stomach.

"Are you hurt?" Jeremy scrambled up, tugging at Sarah's arm to pull her with him.

The passengers inside the coach managed to struggle to their feet, testing their arms and legs as though making sure everything worked.

The door, which was now on top of the coach, was thrown open. Two of the passengers who'd ridden outside reached down to help the others climb out.

When everyone was standing free of the coach, Clint steadied the horses, and the male passengers joined together to heave the coach back onto its wheels.

No one attempted to board the coach. As though they were all a little fearful of trying their luck again, they stood aside, brushing off their rumpled clothing. A few of them grumbled complaints under their breath.

"Get back on," Clint called down from his perch. "We'll need to make up lost time."

Jeremy, the last passenger to get in, paused with one foot inside the coach and one on the brace. "Next time you're going over, give us some warning," he shouted at Clint.

Clint didn't answer. He started the team with such a jolt that Jeremy went sprawling across the seat. He picked himself up in such bad humor that Sarah reached over to pat his hand.

"We'll be in Leadville tomorrow," she said, "and this bumpy ride will be over."

But within a half hour Clint pulled the team to a halt and shouted to his passengers, "Everybody out, but be careful about it. The road's narrow here."

"Narrow" did not fully describe the condition of the road. It hung on the edge of a steep drop, and Sarah didn't dare get close enough to look down at the rocks below. She hurried to the other side of the road, leaning against the rough rock face for support.

She could see why Clint had stopped. A small rock slide lay across the road, and all the passengers struggled to move the larger rocks out of the way so the coach could pass.

A few of the rocks were too large to be budged, but Clint measured the distance across the road with a practiced eye. "I can get the coach through," he said.

Sarah gasped and glanced quickly toward the mountain drop.

"But not with my passengers on it," Clint added. "You stay here, and I'll handle the coach. When I reach the other side of the rock slide, you follow on foot. There's a wide place in the road just beyond this point, and you can get back aboard when we reach it."

The passengers didn't make a sound as Clint climbed back into the driver's seat and slowly, carefully began to maneuver the coach across the narrow passage.

"He can't make it," Sarah heard one of the women whisper, and she held her breath, her heart thumping, as she watched the large back wheels slip closer to the far edge of the road. The front wheels of the coach held, but as the coach swerved around the boulders that blocked part of the way, the right back wheel slid on the gravel and began to dip over the side.

"Hiiahh!" Clint yelled and snapped the reins. The horses gave a spurt, jerking the empty coach up on the roadbed and around the curve ahead.

Sarah put her hands to her heart and let out the breath she'd been holding. With the others she ran forward, eager to see for herself that Clint had brought the coach to safety.

Sarah felt her right foot twist as she stepped on a small, sharp rock. At the same time a heavy body seemed to slam against her, knocking her sideways. Losing her balance on the sloping ground, Sarah fell, clutching desperately for a handhold as she rolled and slid toward the outer edge of the road.

Screams bounced and slammed through Sarah's head. She didn't know if the other women were screaming or the screams were her own. In a dizzying whirl of terror, Sarah pitched over the loose edge of the road, falling off the sheer drop of the mountainside.

Chapter 9

• • •

Something sharp and stiff whipped against Sarah's legs and smashed against her hips. Heedless of the needle-like pain, she grabbed the object and hung on, discovering only when she came to a jolting stop that it was a young pine growing from a crevice in the rock. The branch she clung to bent with her weight, but as she slid downward a few inches, her toes touched something solid.

"Help!" Sarah yelled as the pine wavered and blurred before her. People shouted, but the wild pounding of her heart was so loud in her ears, it drowned out what they were saying. "Help me!" she screamed. She couldn't hold on much longer!

A voice just above her head came through firmly and clearly enough for Sarah to pay attention. "Stop screaming and listen to me," Clint ordered.

"I'm going to fall," Sarah called to him. "I'm going to faint."

"No, you're not," he said. "You're not the fainting

kind, Sarah. You've got enough gumption to hang on till I come down and get you."

In spite of her predicament, all Sarah could think for the moment was, *Gumption? He doesn't know anything about me. What makes him think I've got gumption?*

"There's a narrow rock ledge right beneath you," Clint said. "Slide down the branch just a bit, and you can reach it. It will carry some of your weight. Just don't let go of the branch."

Terrified, Sarah forced herself to shift her hold as Clint had directed. The rough bark of the pine had torn her gloves, and her hands stung with pain, but the rock against her feet was solid and reassuring.

"Here I come," Clint said, and Sarah ducked and squeezed her eyes shut as a shower of pebbles bounced around her.

He spoke from behind her. "Don't let go," he said. "I'm going to tie a rope around your shoulders and chest—kind of a harness—so they can pull you up."

Sarah heard a crack and looked up to see a split in the branch. "It's going to break off!" she cried.

"Never mind," Clint said. "We have time."

She felt the rope around her and winced as it pulled tight; but she couldn't pull her gaze away from the break in the branch. Splinters of new wood, greenish gold, curled downward, stretching . . . stretching . . .

The branch snapped, and Sarah fell backward, her feet slipping from the rock, but Clint's arms were around her, steadying her, and the harness held tightly.

"Brace one foot against the side of the drop and come around to face me," he said.

Gingerly Sarah turned. As she swung out, she saw

the deep drop beneath her feet, and she closed her eyes in panic. Were those mewly little noises coming from her?

"Open your eyes," Clint said, "and do as I say. Wrap your arms around my chest and your legs around my hips."

Shock opened Sarah's eyes. "I can't do that!" she protested, but Clint's deep blue eyes bore into hers.

"Yes, you can," he said, "and you will, if you want to get out of here in one piece. I'll use my legs as springs to keep us from bouncing into the side of the rock as we're pulled up to the road. We're wasting time. Do what I told you. Now."

A sprinkle of pebbles and a sizable rock slammed past Sarah's head. Without another word she wrapped her arms and legs around Clint and held on tightly. He then called out to those on the road, who began to pull upward on the ropes. The ascent was rough, but as Clint had promised, the spring in his knees and elbows kept their bodies from bumping and scraping the side of the mountain cliff.

Suddenly arms grabbed Sarah's shoulders, and Jeremy shouted, "Let go of him, Sarah! We've got you now."

As she obeyed, she was tugged to her feet and pulled away from the edge of the road. Jeremy put an arm around her shoulders, holding her tightly, and tried to hand her the purse she had dropped, but Sarah looked only at Clint, who was brushing the dirt from his clothes.

"Thank you," she said to Clint, then turned to the others. "You all helped. Thank you."

Everyone had something to say about Sarah's ordeal,

but Clint ended the conversation by ordering, "Back on the coach." As most of the passengers walked toward the coach, he stepped up to Sarah and Jeremy. "How did that happen?" Clint asked her.

"It looked as though she tripped," Jeremy said.

Sarah noticed the banker, Mr. Morton, and the woman named Lily hanging back to listen. Should she tell Clint that someone had bumped into her, causing her to fall?

No. She didn't even know who had collided with her, and she couldn't cause trouble by making accusations. It had to have been an accident. No one would purposely want to cause her death. The idea was so frightening, she pushed it away.

"I—I was hurrying. I stepped on a rock and turned my ankle and fell," she said to Clint.

He studied her carefully for a moment, then nodded. "Take your seat in the coach," he said. "You'll have to do your fixin' up along the way."

She saw his smile and took note of her appearance. Her bonnet was askew, a strand of hair had fallen over one shoulder, and there were streaks of dust and dirt on her coat.

But Clint's smile was friendly, not mocking. Sarah smiled at Clint in return, pulled off her torn gloves, and stuffed them into her pocket. "Thank you again for all that you did. You risked your life to save mine."

His smile grew wider. "A feller from China, working down in Denver, told me a custom they've got in his country. You save someone's life, and from then on that life belongs to you."

"This isn't China," Jeremy broke in. He took Sarah's

elbow and steered her toward the coach so rapidly that she had to trot to keep up.

She managed to brush off her coat before climbing into the coach. She had a rip in the seam under one arm, and a tear in the hem; she could repair those in a few minutes with a needle and thread, and her coat would be none the worse for wear.

Embarrassed to be under the watchful gaze of the other passengers inside the coach, Sarah self-consciously rewound her coil of hair, anchored it with the hairpins that were left, and poked her bonnet back into shape. The hatpin had fallen out, but no matter. She tied the blue ribbons firmly under her chin and gazed out the window.

In spite of a few bruises, which were beginning to smart, Sarah wanted to pretend the incident hadn't happened and forget the danger, but Lily and Annie Mae conversed loudly about every accident they'd heard of that had taken place along the road, and apparently there had been many.

The ride during the rest of the day had its harrowing moments. Once the stage rocked crazily onto two wheels, and Sarah braced herself as she saw the passengers on the outside leap to safety, but Clint managed to right the rig before any harm was done. Another time the passengers had to climb out of the coach as Clint backed the team down a narrow stretch to a point where he could pull the coach over and give right of way to a loaded ore wagon going down to Denver.

Sarah welcomed any respite from the jouncing ride that set her teeth on edge, and that evening she gratefully sat on a large boulder outside one of the relay stations and ate the food Jeremy brought to her. The sun was low enough to cast long shadows, and a light breeze sang through the pines, playing the long needles as though they were violin strings.

"How much longer until we reach Leadville?" she asked.

"We'll arrive some time tomorrow afternoon," Jeremy answered. He smiled. "Think you can keep from falling down any mountainsides until then?"

Sarah shivered and wished he hadn't reminded her. It all rushed back: the body slamming into hers, the stumble and fall. If it had been an accident, the person who had bumped her ought to have grabbed for her and tried to keep her from falling.

It was an accident! Sarah told herself, but she knew she wasn't being honest. "I didn't just fall," she said aloud. "Someone pushed me."

Jeremy gave a start, almost dropping the bread in his hands. "What? Who pushed you?" he asked.

"I don't know."

"That's a serious charge. Are you sure?"

"I'm sure," Sarah said. "I tried to convince myself it was an accident, but I know it couldn't have been. Someone tried to kill me."

Jeremy scowled. "It doesn't make sense. Who would have a reason for wanting to kill you, Sarah?"

Again she answered, "I don't know."

Clint spoke up from behind them. "Why didn't you tell me this, Sarah?"

Sarah jumped and stammered, "Clint! I didn't know you were there."

He didn't answer as he came to stand in front of

her. He kept his eyes on Sarah, waiting for her to speak.

"I didn't tell you because I didn't want to cause trouble," she tried to explain.

"You're my passenger," he said. "It's my job to get all my passengers safely to Leadville. If there's a problem, I should be told about it."

"It doesn't make sense," Jeremy said. "We didn't know any of the other passengers until we began this trip. No one would have a reason for wanting to harm Sarah."

Sarah didn't argue the point. Maybe it was better for them to think that Jeremy was right. All she wanted was for the frightening episode to disappear from her mind.

Clint nodded thoughtfully, but he said to Sarah, "All the same, I'll keep an eye on you." His glance flicked toward Jeremy as he added, "Especially since you're traveling on your own."

Jeremy stood and faced Clint. "If Sarah needs protection, I can give it to her."

"Like you did back there on the road?"

Jeremy's face flushed an angry red, and Sarah quickly got to her feet and stood between the two men. "I'm grateful to you both," she said, "but I'm going to have to learn to take care of myself."

"Leadville is a rough town," Clint said. "Can you handle a gun?"

"No," she answered.

"Then I'll teach you to shoot."

Sarah stubbornly shook her head. "I couldn't shoot anyone."

"Not even to save your life?"

This was not something she wanted to think about or talk about. "I'm going to Leadville only to find my father, and then I'm taking him home."

"I'm not sure it's a place you should be at all," Clint told her.

Sarah lifted her chin and stared right into his eyes. "If anyone believes in me, you should," she challenged. "You told me I had gumption."

For a long moment Clint's gaze met Sarah's. Then he said, "Fine. But I'll still teach you how to handle a gun." He turned and strode back to the coach.

Jeremy took Sarah's hand, tucked it protectively in the crook of his elbow, and started toward the coach. "Let's board before the others," he told her. "There's no reason why we should sit across the aisle from each other any longer. From now on, I'm going to sit next to you."

"Won't the ladies complain if you take the middle seat and they can't sit together?"

"You can't be expected to know, Sarah, but those two are not ladies," Jeremy said solemnly.

Sarah knew perfectly well what Jeremy meant. She was certainly old enough to have learned about painted women. "They're still people," she answered, "and they have feelings."

"So do I," Jeremy said. He opened the coach door and held it so that Sarah could climb into the coach first. "And I'm determined to sit next to you."

During the night the coach bumped and wobbled over the rough road, and Sarah was glad that Jeremy had been insistent. In a few exhausted moments of sleep, the ride was cushioned somewhat by his arms around her and his shoulder to rest her head on.

Mr. Fryer snored loudly, and Annie Mae made whistling noises through her teeth as she slept, but Sarah ignored them. When she was not asleep herself, she tugged Jeremy's lap robe up to her chin and kept her eyes on the landscape, which the full moon had frosted with a pure white light.

Sarah was startled when the coach rolled to a stop to find that the moonlight had faded to an early morning gray. They were in the town of Fairplay, where they'd eat a hot breakfast.

Sarah's legs and back ached as she climbed from the coach. How thankful she was for the chance to freshen her appearance! How even more thankful she'd be when they finally arrived in Leadville!

Breakfast was much like those she'd prepared each morning at home, with eggs, beefsteak, potatoes, and thick slices of buttered bread. Although she had to pay seventy-five cents for the meal, Sarah was so hungry that she didn't mind what it cost. After she'd eaten, she took advantage of Jeremy's conversation with Mr. Morton about the effect of the Boer War on international trade to slip outside alone, thankful for a few moments of privacy.

The air was cold and clear and fragrant with pine. Sarah breathed deeply, gulping in the thinner air of the high altitude. She walked carefully across the rutted road, rubbing her hands together. Fortunately her coat was warm enough, but she'd need to purchase new gloves and a scarf—maybe warm boots, as well.

As she turned to walk back, she saw Lily trotting at a fast clip toward her.

"Wait! Please!" Lily called.

Lily paused just a few feet away in the shade of a large oak tree and stood there with one hand on her chest, panting for breath. "Have to get used to it each time I come up here," she said.

Sarah smiled. "It affects me, too." She took a step forward, but Lily held up a hand.

"I got somethin' to tell you," she said, "and I don't want the others to hear." She looked back toward the station. "It's about your father. Your bein' in Leadville can only mean trouble for him."

Sarah's heart gave a jump at the idea that such a woman knew her father. "I'm not going to cause trouble!" she insisted. "I've come only to tell my father that Mother has died and ask him to come back to Chicago with me. I must tell him what has happened. He should know."

"Yes. He should know his wife has died, but someone else could tell him, not you."

"Why not me?" Sarah impatiently demanded. "What are you talking about?"

Lily moved closer. The floral scent with which she had doused herself wasn't enough to hide the bad odor of her body and her sour breath, but Sarah stood firm as the woman lowered her voice and spoke almost in Sarah's ear. "If you search for your father, if you find him . . . it's going to mean his death!"

"What are you talking about?"

Lily ignored Sarah's question and warned, "There might even be those who think enough of Ben to protect him by getting rid of *you*."

"What people? Why should they want to keep me

from my father?" Sarah cried, but Lily glanced back again toward the station, where passengers were beginning to gather.

"I can't explain. Just believe me," she said. She turned and strode toward the stagecoach.

Sarah followed more slowly, trying to make sense of what Lily had said. It wasn't possible that finding Father could mean his death. Or hers.

Or was it? It was highly likely that someone already had tried to get rid of her.

Chapter 10

* * *

As Sarah settled herself inside the coach, again sharing Jeremy's lap robe, she surreptitiously studied the other passengers. Mr. Fryer, the wealthy owner of a number of successful silver and gold mines, seemed to keep to himself. Susannah would have called him a grump. Sarah caught Mr. Morton staring at her, but he quickly looked away when their eyes met. Mr. Morton was a respected banker in the community. Surely neither of these men would want to harm her or her father.

But someone had pushed her over the edge of a cliff.

Lily sat across from Sarah near the window at the far side of the coach, her eyes on the landscape. The muscles around her eyes drooped, and her cheeks sagged. Sarah was sure the woman was much older than she tried to appear, and for a moment she felt sorry for her, but she wondered, *Was it you who pushed me? Why would I be a threat to you?*

Lily had called her father *Ben,* so she must know him, yet Sarah refused to believe that a man like her father would have anything to do with a woman like that. Her father was a hardworking miner, wasn't he? Well . . . wasn't he?

Sarah admitted that she really knew very little about her own father.

The road wound higher into the mountains, and as they crossed Weston Pass, a light snow fell, slowing the progress of the coach. It was freezing inside the coach, and Sarah hated to think how cold it must be for the passengers who rode outside.

Twice more the passengers had to wait at the roadside until Clint steered the horses and empty coach over tricky and dangerous terrain. The second time Sarah stood exhausted in the snow, wishing her toes and hands weren't so cold, telling herself, *I'll be leaving Leadville with Father soon—maybe on the next stage. No more of this high-mountain thin air, no more strange, threatening people. We'll go back to Susannah, to Chicago, to civilization, and everything will be fine again.*

As fine as it could be without Mother.

Sarah's eyes blurred, and a tear rolled down her nose. Quickly she brushed it away, hoping no one had noticed.

Around mid-afternoon they reached the Arkansas River and followed it to the mouth of California Gulch. "Leadville's just a few miles ahead," Clint announced, and Sarah silently rejoiced.

Under the lap robe Jeremy took Sarah's hand in his and stroked her fingers with his thumb. Sarah smiled at him a little shyly as she saw the affection in his eyes; but in her mind she saw Clint's large, rough, callused hands, which gripped the reins, and she hoped they were warm inside his heavy gloves.

The light snow had stopped by the time the big Concord coach entered Leadville. It lumbered down Chestnut Street toward the Grand Hotel. The streets were crowded and noisy with the heavy traffic of ore-loaded wagons being pulled by six- and eight-mule teams, their drivers cracking big bullwhips and shouting at their teams at the tops of their voices. Smaller wagons filled with building materials and supplies, horseback riders, and pedestrians fought for the remaining space.

On either side of the street, behind the uneven, jury rigged, wooden sidewalks, stood rows of buildings, both wooden and brick. Run-down shacks and even some tents occupied an occasional empty space. Nearly every other building seemed to house a saloon, gaming house, or dance hall, and already the music and the voices raised to be heard over it were a din.

Sarah clutched the coach's window frame and stared out at that sea of bustling humanity with a sinking feeling. She didn't know what she'd expected Leadville to be like, but this wasn't it. How was she going to begin to look for her father in such a hodgepodge?

Sarah felt sick. "I didn't imagine what Leadville would be like. I stupidly thought that if I just asked a few people if they knew my father, I'd find one who could direct me to him. Now I don't know where to begin."

"Perhaps my uncle can help through *The Leadville Daily Star*," Jeremy suggested.

"A sound idea," Mr. Morton said. "A newspaper reaches everyone. By all means keep Chester Caulfield in mind."

Mr. Fryer suddenly looked up and surprised Sarah by

92

grumbling, "You don't need any of the newspapers. Try the courthouse. Last spring the council commissioned a census of sorts, making an effort to list all the residents."

"How many were there?" Sarah began to be hopeful.

"Five thousand and forty of 'em," he answered. "However, it's suspected that another five thousand or so live outside of town near mine sites and such."

"Ten thousand people!"

"From late spring on it's closer to twenty, and more will come in and out of town afore the bad weather shuts down the pass in a month or two."

Sarah fell against Jeremy as the coach pulled to a sudden stop. The door was thrown open, and she picked herself up and struggled to the doorway, preparing to climb down. But this time Clint encircled her waist with his hands and lifted her over the frozen ruts in the street, setting her down on the wooden sidewalk.

"Stay there and don't move," he said. "Someone else will take care of the coach and horses, so as soon as I unload the bags, I'll be free to take you to a place I know about."

"Now just a minute," Jeremy protested. He stood close by Sarah's side.

Clint faced him, almost nose to nose. "Do you know of a good clean boardinghouse hereabouts where a young woman would be safe?"

"Well, I . . . no," Jeremy said.

"I do," Clint said. He climbed to the top of the coach and began handing down bags to the passengers. The last one was Sarah's, and he kept a firm grip on it. "The boardinghouse I have in mind is just a few streets over," he explained. "There's a nice widow woman named Mary Hannigan running it. It'll be faster getting there if we walk."

"I'll go with you," Jeremy insisted.

Before Clint could answer, Sarah asked Jeremy, "What about your uncle? Won't he be coming to meet you?"

"No," Jeremy said. "Uncle Chester wrote that meeting me would be difficult. He just gave me directions to his house on Fourth Street and said it was a short walk." His chin jutted out stubbornly. "I intend to make sure that Sarah is in good hands before I leave her."

Sarah walked down Harrison Avenue between the two men, her eyes on the ground in front of her to keep from falling. Each businessman had built his own section of sidewalk as an adjunct to his building, so that each walkway was at a different height from those on either side. With the crush of people on the streets, it was hard not to stumble over the drops and lifts, which were anywhere from an inch to a foot's difference.

As they crossed State Street, dodging the carts, wagons, and other pedestrians, the din became even louder. "Stay away from this street," Clint said, and this time his glance included Jeremy, too. "Along this stretch are the worst of the gamblers—crooks and bunco artists every one of 'em, and—um—well, other forms of vice." Quickly he added, "And in a crowd like that, you'll come up against plenty of footpads."

"What are footpads?" Sarah asked.

"Pickpockets, thieves, armed robbers." Sarah could hear the contempt in Clint's voice.

"But we saw saloons and dance halls on Chestnut Street as we drove into town," Sarah said.

"There are more than a hundred saloons in town, but the *worst* are on State Street," Clint said. He slowed his pace a little, for which Sarah was thankful. "But you're right. The other main streets can be dangerous, too. There are plenty of men who made money from finding veins of silver and gold and deposits of lead carbonate, and they got nowhere to go to spend it except in the theaters and the gambling halls and the Leadville saloons. Even those miners who are working for three dollars a day, ten hours a day, six days a week, want a place to come just to get out of the miserable shacks they live in. This town's a gambler's paradise." He glanced again at Jeremy. "I hope you own a gun."

"A new Remington Frontier, forty-four caliber," Jeremy said proudly.

"Its balance isn't as good as a Colt's," Clint answered. He glanced at Jeremy's hip. "Where is it?"

"In my satchel."

"Wear it," Clint said.

Sarah didn't like the expression on Jeremy's face. Trying to change the subject, she asked Clint, "You said there are theaters in Leadville?"

"Some have acts you wouldn't want to see," Clint told her, "but Tom Kemp's Grand Central Theater brings in some good troupes. Right now they're playing Shakespeare. Eddie Foy brought his vaudeville here a couple of months ago, and Horace Tabor's got an opera house under construction."

As they passed Third Street and Fourth Street—there were no street signs, but Clint was familiar with the town—Sarah saw a number of cabins and tidy wooden houses, many of them painted. There were some larger homes, with neatly tended front lawns and shrubs on Fourth Street, and she wondered which one might belong to Jeremy's uncle.

They walked down Fifth Street, a quiet row of two-story houses. Clint turned up the walk to a neat house painted white with blue trim, and Sarah felt a surge of hope.

Mrs. Hannigan, a stout, round, and rosy-cheeked woman in a plain black dress with a white lace collar, answered the door. The fragrance of meat stew or soup wafted around her, and Sarah's stomach clutched with hunger. Mrs. Hannigan greeted Clint with a welcoming smile and, as Clint introduced Sarah and Jeremy, invited them all inside her parlor.

"Oh!" Sarah exclaimed as she sat down and surveyed the room with its heavily carved furniture, plush upholstery, crocheted doilies on the arms and backs of the chairs, and floral and scenic paintings. "This is so much like our home!"

"Tell me about your home, dear," Mrs. Hannigan encouraged, and Sarah found herself describing not only her home, but even some of the boarders. She told this motherly woman about her mother's death, Uncle Amos and Aunt Cora's acquisition of everything Mother had owned, and Susannah's plan to send Sarah to Leadville.

As Sarah finished the story, she was surprised to find that her cheeks were wet. Embarrassed, she reached into her coat pocket for a clean handkerchief. As she pulled it out, the torn gloves came with it, falling to her feet.

"You poor, dear child!" Mrs. Hannigan indignantly picked up the gloves, patting them as though with a bit of tender care she could restore them. "I've got a nice little room upstairs in the back that should suit you while you're in Leadville. I can let you have it for nine dollars a week, and that includes three meals a day."

Nine dollars! Sarah gulped and mentally counted the money left in the packet. Aware that Mrs. Hannigan was waiting for an answer, Sarah quickly said, "Thank you. I'll pay you in advance, as soon as . . . as I get my . . . uh . . . things together." Mrs. Hannigan nodded agreement, and Sarah said, "I probably won't be here for a full week. Father and I will have to go back to Chicago as soon as possible."

"You might talk to our marshal, Pat Kelly," Mrs. Hannigan suggested. "He hasn't had the job long and wouldn't know everyone in town, the way our good Marshal Martin Duggan did, but there's still a chance he might have heard of your father."

In spite of her exhaustion, Sarah perked up. "That makes three places to begin—the marshal, the court-house, and Mr. Caulfield's newspaper, *The Leadville Daily Star.*"

"You'll need to give people a description of your father," Clint said. "Do you remember what he looks like?"

Clint was the first person who'd asked that question, and it took Sarah by surprise. She could clearly remember Father as he was ten years ago, but she had no idea how time might have changed him. "He's a tall man," she answered. "Mother said I take after him, not only in being tall, but in many ways. His hair's the same color as mine."

"Dark red," Clint said.

"Auburn," Jeremy corrected.

"And our eyes are the same color."

"Sort of a yellow brown," Clint said.

"Golden." Jeremy glared at Clint.

"But I mostly remember he laughed easily and was full of fun. His eyes sparkled with mischief. He'd do the most marvelous card tricks for me—and fool me every time."

"You played cards in your household?" Mrs. Hannigan's eyebrows rose like warning signs.

"Oh, no," Sarah said. "Mother didn't allow card games in the house. She didn't even like Father's card tricks. She firmly believed that playing cards are wicked."

Mrs. Hannigan nodded with satisfaction.

A fair-haired young woman dressed in a starched white shirtwaist and dark blue skirt entered the room. "Ah! Here's Miss Elsie Landerman, one of our teachers," Mrs. Hannigan said, and got to her feet. She quickly performed the introductions, then said, "It's time to stir up a batch of biscuits. The stew will be ready as soon as they're baked. Elsie, will you please take Sarah up to the room at the end of the hall?"

Mrs. Hannigan deftly ushered Jeremy and Clint to the door and out to the porch.

"I'll come back tonight," Jeremy called to Sarah.

"Not tonight," Mrs. Hannigan told him. "Can't you see that the poor girl is nearly asleep on her feet?"

She closed the door and shooed Sarah and Elsie toward the stairs before she trotted toward the kitchen.

"Will you be here long?" Elsie asked Sarah as she led the way down the upstairs hall.

"Only until I find my father," Sarah answered. She

saw the curiosity in Elsie's eyes, but she was too tired to go through the story again.

At the end of the hall, Elsie stepped ahead of Sarah and opened a door that led to a small spare bedroom. A narrow single bed, covered with a white cotton spread, stood against the far wall. Under the window was a small upholstered chair. On Sarah's left was a narrow wardrobe and beyond it a dresser, which held, upon a pair of crocheted doilies, a pitcher and bowl and a hand-painted oil lamp. Two woven rag rugs, made from multicolored dark strips of cloth, decorated the scrubbed and polished wooden floor. The room was comfortable. It looked like home, and Sarah put down her carpetbag with a sigh of relief.

A skinny child, no older than nine or ten, staggered into the room with a full pitcher of water.

"Let me help you," Sarah said, and took the pitcher from her, pouring the water into her own pitcher. She handed the empty pitcher back to the child.

"Thank you, miss," the girl said. "My name is Mollie. You want anything, you just let me know."

She ran from the room before Sarah could answer, and Elsie smiled. "Mollie is Mrs. Hannigan's current helper. There's quite a turnover." She added, "Your coat is torn. I've got a needle and thread in my room. I'll bring them in a minute."

Sarah pulled off her coat and slumped on the edge of the bed. True to her word Elsie returned quickly and laid the items on the dresser.

Sarah sleepily tried to think of something to chat about, but Elsie walked from the doorway out into the hall. "You've got about fifteen minutes before supper. I'll see you then."

The cold water Sarah splashed on her face and neck helped to keep her awake. She was tempted to skip supper and fall into bed, but her stomach was aching with hunger. Sarah didn't bother to unpack. She quickly stitched the ripped seam and torn hem in her coat and hung it in the wardrobe. Then she unbuttoned her blouse and wiggled and squirmed until she had tugged the packet from its place of safety. With a sigh she removed a ten-dollar greenback.

It was impossible to return the packet to its protected spot inside her corset without undoing the corset, so she tucked it under her camisole above the snug waistband of her skirt.

Sarah found her own way to the dining room, joining the others just as they were taking seats around the large table. She met the other boarders, all of them respectable-looking men, but she was unable to remember most of their names. The gentleman next to her, Mr. Milton Vonachek, was tall and pleasant looking, with thin blond hair and a long moustache with waxed, curled ends. Through the meal he tried to entertain Sarah with amusing stories about some of the inhabitants of Leadville.

Sarah appreciated his efforts but paid little attention as she ate slowly and steadily, barely able to keep herself from wolfing down the fragrant stew and the steaming hot biscuits. When the others rose from the table, after the last scrap of the good food had been eaten, Sarah wandered with them into the living room.

"It's an early bedtime for you, Sarah," Mrs. Hannigan ordered, but a knock at the door drew their attention. The door was opened, and Clint came into the living room.

"I've got something to tell Sarah," he said to Mrs. Hannigan. "It's about her father."

Sarah's desire for sleep disappeared in a rush. She ran to Clint's side and begged, "Oh, please! Tell me now. Have you found him?"

Clint paused, looking around at the faces that were turned toward him. "What I have to say is kind of private."

"Then go into the dining room where the lamps are still lit," Mrs. Hannigan suggested. "You can close the sliding doors if you wish. Mollie may be clearing the table, but pay her no mind."

Sarah led the way, and as soon as they were in the room, she tugged the doors together, heedless of Mollie, who was at the other end of the room carrying plates to the kitchen. "You've found him already? Where is he?" Sarah cried.

Clint clamped a hand on her shoulder as though he were holding her in place. "I haven't found your father," he said. "But I've got some information about him."

"What is it?" Sarah bounced impatiently. "Oh, please don't keep me waiting! What do you know?"

Clint leaned close and lowered his voice. "Listen to me, Sarah," he said.

Sarah was vaguely aware that Mollie had stopped her travels from table to kitchen and back again and was standing still, plates in hand.

"The way you described your father, I couldn't think of him as being a miner, working hard for low wages," Clint said. "What you told us about your father being so good with card tricks got me to thinking, so I asked around, and I found a man who knew Ben Lindley and what he did for a living." Clint took a deep breath before he went on. "You're going to have to face up to something you may not like, Sarah. Your father wasn't a miner. He was a gambler."

Sarah backed up, groped for a chair, and plopped into it. Clint pulled another chair close and sat facing her, taking her hands into his.

"Are you all right?" he asked.

"Yes," Sarah said.

"Would you like some water?" He looked up. "There was a girl here. . . ." But Mollie had skedaddled.

"I don't need anything to drink," Sarah told him. She looked up into Clint's eyes and was surprised to recognize a tenderness and concern that seemed so unlike his direct, sometimes blunt nature. Taking a deep breath, she sat a little straighter and said, "But I do need more of an explanation. You said my father *was* a gambler. Are you telling me that my father is dead?"

Clint shook his head. "No, no. I said *was* because the man I talked to did. Your father seems to be well-known in these parts, but this man hasn't seen your father around town for over two weeks. Nobody has."

Chapter 11

• • •

Sarah waited, watching Clint's face. He went on. "That doesn't mean much. Maybe he moved on to another town."

"But you don't think so, do you? I want the truth, Clint."

"The feeling is that he's still somewhere around these parts. That's all I know, Sarah. That *is* the truth."

She clung to his hands. "Was Father . . . one of those crooked gamblers on that awful street you told us about—State Street?"

"No." Clint spoke more easily now. "Matter of fact, he was described to me as a good dresser—pearl stickpin, polished boots, and all—and he worked out of two of the better places in town, Owens's Faro Club and the Texas House. I don't know anybody at either of them, but I could go 'round and ask about him."

Sarah's head began to hurt, and she pulled her hands away and pressed them against her forehead. "I'm too tired to think right now," she said, "and I know how tired you must be, too. At least I was able to get a few moments of sleep on the coach, but you had to drive straight through."

"That's part of the job. It isn't so bad," Clint said, but Sarah could see the hollows under his eyes.

"Will you have to drive the stage back tomorrow?" she asked.

"No," he said. "I'll have a day off before I go back. I . . ." He cleared his throat and started again. "I'd like to see you again, Sarah. I'd like to come calling."

Come calling? It sounded as if Clint intended to court her. Surely not. He knew she'd be going back to Chicago soon. Sarah wasn't sure what to say or do, so she simply nodded *yes*.

"Tomorrow morning?"

"Morning will be fine. Later I want to go to that Faro Club or the Texas House and talk to the people there. Someone must know where my father has gone."

Clint's jaw tightened. "You don't belong there, Sarah. Any talking that needs to be done around those places will be done by me and not you."

"You said they were two of the better places in town."

His face grew red. "That's right, but they're still not fitting places for a lady to set foot in."

"People might be more likely to talk to me instead of you because Ben Lindley is my father."

"No," he said stubbornly. "I want you to stay away from those places."

We'll see about that! Sarah thought. She'd come a long distance to find her father, and she was not about to sit back and let some brave protector take over. She

104

was more determined than ever to get Father out of this terrible situation and back to Chicago.

Into Sarah's mind came the words she'd wailed to Susannah: "I can't go! I can't face that awful unknown country!" A smile flickered at the corners of her mouth. Susannah should see her now.

Clint took the smile as an expression of agreement, and his expression softened. As he got to his feet, he said, "I'll be back tomorrow morning, Sarah."

She walked Clint to the front door, then turned around and said good night to all the curious people in the room. They were all kind, friendly people, she was sure, but for now they were no more real to her than portraits on a wall. She longed for the privacy of her room so she could think things out, and she desperately needed to sleep.

Even after she had washed her face, hands, and arms and had pulled her nightgown over her head, her mind was still in a turmoil. *I'll never be able to close my eyes,* she thought, but by the time her body heat had begun to weave a warm cocoon under the thick quilt, Sarah was drifting into sleep.

In the morning, after a hearty breakfast, Sarah asked Mrs. Hannigan if she could purchase a sheet of paper and an envelope and have the use of pen and ink, so that she could write a letter to her sister.

Mrs. Hannigan obliged with what Sarah needed and gave directions to the post office, where she could buy a three-cent stamp.

All the other boarders had left for work, so Sarah

settled herself in a sunny spot under an east window in the parlor and began her letter to her sister. *Dear Susannah*, she wrote, then paused. Should she tell her about meeting Jeremy and Clint? About the train robbery and the thief in the hotel? Should she tell her what the terrible town of Leadville was really like? She shuddered. How could she dash Susannah's hopes by telling her what she had discovered so far about their father?

She pictured her little sister's smiling face, her pretty brown hair and eyes that snapped with an alert no-nonsense manner. Oh, how terribly she missed Susannah! Sarah's chest began to ache, and her throat grew tight.

Writing to Susannah wasn't enough. She wanted to hear from her sister that everything was all right and that Mr. Abrams was looking out for her welfare. She wanted to hug Susannah and hold her tightly and assure her that Uncle Amos and Aunt Cora would never bother them again.

But she couldn't.

With determination she dipped her pen point in the ink bottle again, wiping it against the side to get rid of any extra drops that might blot the paper, and wrote:

After a long and tiring trip, I have arrived in Leadville and have taken residence at Mrs. Mary Hannigan's boardinghouse on Fifth Street. I have met some very kind people who have promised to help me find Father. Apparently Father was in Leadville until about two weeks ago, so it is fair to expect that he will return soon. I hope that it will take only a short time to find him. When I do, and our plans are made for the trip back to Chicago, I will write to you immediately.

I miss you, dearest sister, and I love you with all my heart.

Sarah

She folded the paper, put it into the envelope, and addressed the letter to Mr. Abrams, at the Lindleys' boardinghouse address on Wabash Avenue. He'd make sure that Susannah got it.

Clint arrived shortly after, and Sarah, who found herself unaccountably shy, ushered him into the parlor. His trousers and jacket had been brushed clean, the flannel shirt he wore looked new and still a little stiff, and she could smell the same Bay Rum fragrance on his skin that Mr. Abrams sometimes used. Clint held a small package, and Sarah wondered if it was a gift.

She perched on the edge of a chair, and Clint sat uncomfortably on a sofa opposite her.

"I'm glad the sun is out," Sarah said. "It should be a lovely day."

Clint cleared his throat, said, "Yep. Leadville's weather . . ." He broke off, shaking his head. "I'm not good at this kind of talk," he told her. "I say what I think, and I don't think much about weather, unless I'm in it, and then I'm usually cursin' it."

He thrust the package at her, and Sarah smiled. "What's in it?"

"I told you what I was going to bring you. Open it."

Sarah pulled off the string and brown paper and opened the box inside, discovering a small handgun and a box containing ammunition. "Not a gun!" Sarah cried.

"It's a Colt pocket derringer, forty-one caliber," Clint said. "It'll fit in that little purse of yours and be there handy if you need it."

Sarah continued to shrink back from the shining, deadly thing on her lap. "I wouldn't know what to do with it."

"You will, soon enough." Clint stood and took the package from Sarah. "Come on," he said. "Get your coat. I've got a couple of horses outside."

"I've never been on a horse."

"You'll learn. The one I brought for you is a gentle mare, and I've got her fixed up with a sidesaddle." He waited a moment, while Sarah continued to sit on the chair as though she were bolted to it, before he spoke up again. "I said you had gumption, Sarah. I don't think I was wrong."

Sarah jumped to her feet. "Of course I have gumption. I was just thinking about what you asked me to do and deciding whether or not I would do it. I'll learn to ride a horse, because that might be a useful thing to know; but I am not going to learn how to shoot someone."

"Where's your coat?" he asked. "I brought a pair of woolen gloves for you. They might be too big, but they'll keep your hands warm."

Sarah ran to get her coat and hat, pulled on the gloves, and followed Clint outside to the street where two saddled horses were hitched to a ring in a post. As Clint and Sarah approached, the brown one with the black mane rolled his eyes and tossed his head. Sarah jumped back and smothered a yelp.

"Yours is Lady, the quiet one," Clint said. "Samson is mine." He put Sarah's package in the saddlebags on the brown horse, talking low and stroking the horse's neck as he did so. He moved to the smaller white-and-black mare and held out a hand to Sarah. "Over here," he directed.

Hoping her fear didn't show on her face, Sarah managed to walk to Clint's side. He laced his fingers together, bent over, and began to give instructions. "Step on my hand with your left foot."

Sarah did and found herself being boosted into the air.

"Here—bend your right leg around that curved horn on the left side and sit comfortable while I slip your left foot into the stirrup," Clint said.

Gingerly Sarah settled into the saddle, and Clint handed her the reins, saying, "I'll keep a lead rein on Lady, but you'll soon learn to guide her."

"L-Lady," Sarah said shakily, and patted the horse who took a few quick steps sideways.

Clint unhitched Samson and swung into the saddle. Keeping the pair of horses at a walk, Clint led them away from the main streets of town. After a block or two, the residential side streets came to an end, and they rode a trail through rolling meadow grasses that wound between stands of pine. Beyond them a towering range of snowcapped mountains glistened in the sunlight, and Sarah, soothed by the beauty surrounding her, began to enjoy the rhythmic rocking motion of her horse.

Clint instructed Sarah in the use of the reins and showed her how to use the pressure of her left foot to guide her horse. He then unfastened the lead and told her to try it on her own. Lady obeyed perfectly, and Sarah looked up and laughed with delight at Clint, who rode next to her.

Clint suddenly spurred his horse to a trot, and Lady followed suit. Sarah let out a squeak, and Clint called to her, "You're all right. Just keep your balance and don't let those reins go slack. In a minute we'll go into a canter."

"I don't think I'm ready."

"Sure you are. Don't be afraid. I'm right here with you."

When they reached a small grove of trees and pulled their horses to a stop, Sarah patted Lady's neck again and admitted, "When I got over being frightened, I liked it."

"I knew you would. Now that you know what you're doing, you can ride Lady anytime you want to. I'll tell them down at the stables." Clint swung off Samson, fastened the reins of both horses to a small sapling, and reached up to lift Sarah from Lady. He took the package from his saddlebags, opened it, and lifted out the gun.

"No," Sarah told him.

"You never have to use this, Sarah," Clint said. "I'm just asking you to learn how." He paused and added, "Please do this for me."

Clint didn't look like the kind of man who used the word please very often. The way he was looking at her, so hopeful, so caring . . . Sarah nodded. "Very well," she said. "I'll learn to use it. That's all I'll promise."

"That's enough." Clint led her away from the horses

and showed her how to handle the gun safely. Next he showed her how to sight and cock it, and finally he loaded the chamber and put the small Colt into her right hand.

"See that broken limb hanging from the pine over there?" he asked. "Aim for it. See if you can hit it."

Sarah raised the gun, took sight at the target, and squeezed the trigger. The sound made her jump, and she held the gun as far away from her side as she could, the end of the barrel pointing at the ground.

"Look at that!" Clint said proudly. "You skinned the bark on the right side. I didn't expect you to get that close the first time. Now try it again and do even better. Or do you think that was a lucky fluke?"

"I'm going to hit it right in the middle," Sarah informed him. She carefully sighted again and again, missing twice, and coming close once. On her last shot she hit the middle of the branch. "I did it!" she cried.

Clint took his gun from the holster he wore on his right hip. The gun looked huge compared to the one he'd given her, and she wondered how he could handle anything so long and heavy.

"It's a Colt Peacemaker," Clint said. He checked the chamber and placed the gun back in its holster.

"Peacemaker!" she exclaimed, but almost before she could get the word out, Clint drew the gun and fired again and again into the branch, which splintered and crashed to the ground.

He holstered the Peacemaker and said, "I wasn't just trying to show off. You need to understand that in a tight situation there won't be any time to waste. If a man's going for his gun, you have to be faster. You can't take time to steady your aim. You pull your gun, you aim from memory, and you pull the trigger."

"I said I wasn't going to use this gun to shoot anyone!"

"And I said you don't have to. Now load the chamber yourself, and let's see how fast you can learn to draw."

After a number of rounds, Sarah discovered that she could move faster and actually hit the target. When it was a broken branch or a piece of deadwood, the draw and shoot was like a game.

Finally Clint said, "I'd better get you back to Mrs. Hannigan's. If you don't mind, we can take the horses right to the stable, where I keep them, and I'll walk you home from there."

As he helped Sarah into the saddle, she said, "This was a wonderful morning, Clint."

"You're a good student," he said.

They rode back across the meadow, and Sarah urged him to tell her more about the ranch he wanted.

"I lost my parents when I was almost too young to remember them, so I never had a real home," Clint said. His eyes gleamed as he described the land he had in mind to buy. It was north of Denver, and it sloped from the foothills east of the mountains, protected from the worst of the winter storms by the high peaks. He glanced at Sarah as he added, "It will be a good place to build a house, to bring a wife, to raise a family."

Sarah quickly changed the subject, but as they reached Mrs. Hannigan's porch, Clint said, "I have to take tomorrow's run to Denver. That means I won't be back in Leadville for five days, maybe six."

"If I find Father—" she began, but Clint interrupted.

"Wait for me, Sarah. I'll help you find him."

"I can't promise that."

He sighed. "You're a stubborn woman."

"Let's see," Sarah said. "You've told me that I've got gumption, and now that I'm stubborn. One's a compliment, I suppose, but the other . . ."

"The other is, too," he said. "I don't know how it is in city life, but stubbornness is going to serve you well in the West."

Mrs. Hannigan appeared at the door, and Sarah, clutching the box with the gun and ammunition he'd given her, reluctantly left Clint.

"That other young man, the one whose uncle publishes *The Leadville Daily Star*," Mrs. Hannigan said. "He was here twice and finally left you a note."

Sarah read Jeremy's note, smiling at the impatience in his words as he told her he'd been put to work immediately by his uncle. He extended an invitation from his uncle and aunt for dinner that night. He'd pick Sarah up at seven.

Good, Sarah thought. She had been eager to meet Jeremy's uncle and aunt ever since Jeremy had told her that his uncle and his newspaper might be able to help find Father.

She needed to do some things first, however. As soon as she'd enjoyed Mrs. Hannigan's noon meal of roast chicken, squash, and some kind of boiled greens, Sarah ran upstairs to put on her coat again, making sure there was enough money in her reticule with which to purchase a scarf, gloves, warm boots, and a new bonnet. She hefted her umbrella, pleased with the weight of the handle.

Downstairs, ready to go, Sara told Mrs. Hannigan of her plans.

"The Palace of Fashion is a fine shop with a good and reasonable selection of women's clothing. It's on Chestnut Street, next to the Windsor Hotel," Mrs. Hannigan said. "It shouldn't be hard to find."

Sarah just nodded. She had no intention of telling Mrs. Hannigan that she planned another stop—to the Texas House, where she had some inquiries to make.

It took only a few minutes to mail her letter to Susannah and find the things she needed. The bonnet she liked best was a deep blue, trimmed with a pink velvet rose and ribbons to match, and Sarah examined it in the mirror with pleasure. Jeremy would like it. Clint would like it. *She* would like it. "I'll wear it," she told the clerk. "The other things, too."

She stopped at the corner of Chestnut and Harrison to buy ink, pen, and writing paper at a stationery store, then made her way to the Texas House, which was also on Chestnut Street and closer than Owens's Faro Club.

The entire town of Leadville was noisy, but as she drew closer to the gambling house, the din seemed to increase. Sarah walked under the awning of the Texas House and through the front doors and was met by a blast of piano music that made her wince. Although it was early in the afternoon, there was already a great deal of activity in the finely furnished room, which was crowded with table after table of card players. Against the wall was an ornate bar, and some of the drinkers turned to stare at Sarah as she stood in the doorway.

There were not many women in the room—mostly a few in aprons who were carrying drinks to the tables—so when a woman dressed in red turned from the bar to stare at her, Sarah noted her immediately.

"Lily!" Sarah cried out as she recognized her, but Lily turned her back on Sarah and hurried out of the room through a door at the rear.

Sarah, embarrassed at being the center of so much unwelcome attention, clutched her umbrella and parcel tightly, stared straight ahead with her chin held high, and followed Lily.

Sarah found herself in a hallway leading to offices along the side and a back door, which stood open. There was no sign of Lily, but two men dressed in high style, their waistcoats decorated with gold watch chains, stopped their conversation to stare at her.

"Are you looking for someone in particular?" the stout man asked, and Sarah could see that he was puzzled. Clint had been right. She didn't belong here.

Well, no matter, Sarah thought. *I'm here now, so I may as well make the best of the situation.* "Where is Lily?" she asked.

"Lily's busy," the tall man said.

"I didn't come to see Lily," Sarah said, hating the curiosity in his face. "I'm here because I'm searching for my father, Benjamin Lindley."

The two men glanced at each other before the tall one answered abruptly, "He's not here."

"Where is he? Do you know?"

"No," he answered.

He turned to leave, but Sarah pleaded, "Please! I've come such a long distance to find my father. My mother has died, and I must tell Father."

The tall man left without answering, but the stout man studied Sarah. "You're out of luck," he said.

Chills shivered down Sarah's backbone. The man frightened her, and his words were terrifying. "Why do you say that?" she demanded. "Where is my father? What's happened to him?"

The man tugged down his creeping waistcoat and stared at her out of pale eyes as cold as the wind in the mountain passes. "Apparently you don't know, young lady," he said, "your father is an outlaw. He's killed a man and is on the run."

Chapter 12

◆ ◆ ◆

The small amount of courage she had left vanished as the stout man entered an office and closed the door. Sarah didn't dare to make that long walk through the gaming room of the Texas House again. She picked up her skirts and ran out the open back door and down the steps. Once outside, in the debris-filled alley, she leaned against the building, her legs so wobbly she needed the support.

Father an outlaw! A murderer! She couldn't believe a story like that.

"Hsssst!"

Startled, Sarah turned to see a white-aproned girl make sure the door was shut, then run down the steps to join Sarah.

"I'll be in terrible trouble if they find I've left my post," she said, "but I have to talk to you. I'm Bessie— Mollie's sister."

It took a moment for Sarah to remember. "Oh, yes. Little Mollie who works for Mrs. Hannigan."

"That's right. She told me you were looking for your father."

Sarah's eyes welled with tears. "A man I just spoke to told me that Father is an outlaw, that he murdered a man."

"That was Mr. Wilbur Owens. He's not with the Texas House. He owns Owens's Faro Club."

But Sarah was still in shock. She cried out, "I don't believe Father could do it! I don't believe it!"

Bessie took Sarah's shoulders and shook her. "Be quiet and listen to me," she said. "I know what Mr. Owens told you, and that's why I'm takin' the risk of talkin' to you." She dropped her hands, and Sarah could see that there were tears in Bessie's eyes, too.

"Your father was a good man," Bessie said, "no matter what you might hear about him. He shot in self-defense. I saw it. So did plenty others."

"Then why are they calling my father a murderer?"

"That's the least of his worries." Bessie sighed and rubbed her eyes with the back of one hand. "Go back to Chicago," she said. "Your being here can only hurt him."

"That's what Lily told me. What do you mean?"

"You talked to Lily, too?"

"On the stagecoach."

"Listen to us. Go home. Now."

Bessie turned to leave, but Sarah grabbed her arm. "Can't you tell me more about my father?"

"No!"

"Then at least tell me this. Why are you warning me away?"

Bessie thought a moment, then said quietly, "Ben is a

kind and generous man. He helped my family survive last winter after my father was hurt bad in the mines."

"And Lily?"

"Ben once risked his life to save hers. She vowed she'd always be grateful for what he'd done, and I know she'd risk her own life if it came to a matter of savin' Ben's."

Sarah released her grip on Bessie's arm, and Bessie ran to the steps. She turned before opening the door and said to Sarah, "Lily's not like me. All I can do is try to warn you away, but there's no telling what Lily might do to keep you from putting your father's life in danger."

"What danger? You haven't explained what you mean," Sarah persisted. "You have a father, so you must understand how I feel about mine!"

Bessie hesitated. Then she said, "There are others who'd like to know where your father is, too, and that's all I can say."

"Wait!" Sarah cried. "If my father were far away from here, you and Lily wouldn't be so worried. That must mean he's hiding somewhere nearby." She stared into Bessie's eyes. "*You* know where he is, don't you?"

Bessie gave Sarah a sorrowful last look and ran inside, shutting the door firmly behind her.

At least Sarah knew Father *was* alive, in or near Leadville. She hadn't come all this way for nothing. She was determined to find him, and if those people who were warning her to give up and go home thought she'd follow their advice, they'd soon find out they were wrong!

Sarah angrily stomped across a pile of torn papers and rubble and headed past a row of privies toward the nearest side street. She kicked a broken crate out of her way, furious at everyone who was trying to keep her from her father, even furious with the town of Leadville for being filthy and smelly and noisy.

"Turn around and toss me your purse," a deep voice said behind her.

With her parcel in her left hand, Sarah shifted the umbrella in her right so that she held it near the tip, and whirled to face the man. She didn't stop to see what he looked like; she didn't care. She had only a blurred impression of a battered felt hat, a dirty jacket and trousers, and a gun—one as large as Clint's—aimed in her direction. She brought the knobbed end of her umbrella down with a crack across the wrist that held the gun.

He let out a yell of pain, and she swung again, this time connecting with his head. As he staggered back, bouncing off the side of the building, Sarah turned, picked up her skirts, and ran, but he was faster than she was.

Strong arms twisted her around and threw her to the ground. At the same time the man snatched both her umbrella and the purse from her arm. Sarah could only sit there watching helplessly as he fished through her purse, scowling as he pulled his hand from the reticule. "One silver dollar? That's all you've got?"

"That's all," Sarah answered.

"Warn't worth the aggravation," he muttered. He kept the dollar but threw the purse into Sarah's lap, then bent his knee and broke her umbrella across it. As he tossed the torn, bent umbrella to one side of the alley he said, "This is gonna happen again. If you know what's good for you, you'll get out of Leadville."

He turned and ran, and Sarah watched as he suddenly ducked out of the alley—near the Texas House, maybe, but Sarah couldn't be sure.

She got to her feet, dusting off her clothes and new gloves. The items in her parcel appeared undamaged, but the umbrella was in a hopeless state. She might as well leave it where the man had thrown it.

Attacked by a footpad! Clint had warned that she could be. In a rough, unruly town like this, she probably should have expected it to happen; but as she made her way to the street, walking back toward Mrs. Hannigan's boardinghouse, Sarah began to think differently about it.

He wasn't just a footpad, Sarah concluded. *He warned me to leave Leadville, and no ordinary thief would bother to tell me that. Someone must have instructed him to say it—someone who wanted to frighten me. Bessie? No, I don't think so. Lily? Maybe.* Sarah walked a little faster.

When she reached the boardinghouse, Mrs. Hannigan met her at the door. "My, my, I do like that bonnet. It's very becoming," she said.

Before Sarah could acknowledge the compliment, Mrs. Hannigan reached into a pocket of her skirt and pulled out a slip of paper to hand to Sarah. "One of my boarders, Milton Vonachek—the thin man with the elegant moustache, if you remember from last night—works in the courthouse. I asked him to look up an address for Benjamin Lindley, and he brought it to me a few minutes ago. Your father lives in a rooming house, fourth from the corner on Second Street, the other side of Harrison Avenue. You won't find any house numbers, even though the council's after us to start using them. Nobody bothers."

Sarah clutched the piece of paper, looking at the neat handwriting. Father's address. A starting place. "Oh, thank you!" she cried, and impulsively hugged Mrs. Hannigan.

"There's no time for you to go there now, if you want to be ready for dinner with the Caulfields," Mrs. Hannigan said, somewhat taken aback. "And I'd suggest that before you leave to go socializing, you give that coat of yours a good going over. I'll give you a clothes brush to use on it. How it keeps getting so dusty is beyond me."

Sarah didn't explain. She tucked her father's address into her purse, took the brush from Mrs. Hannigan, and went upstairs to get ready. Her peach-colored dress with the lace collar—she'd wear it again tonight.

Jeremy's Uncle Chester was a large, broad-shouldered man with a long, drooping salt-and-pepper moustache and a florid complexion that deepened and lightened through various shades of red, depending on how affected he was by each topic of conversation. His wife, Violet, on the other hand, was every bit as retiring as the flower for which she was named. It was as though her husband had drained her of all color, needing more than his own share. Pale hair, pale skin, pale clothing, Violet Caulfield looked as though she were gradually fading away.

The Caulfields' three-story wooden house was unprepossessing on the outside, but the rooms within were ornamented with massive furniture, glittering chandeliers, countless paintings in gilt frames, embroidered pillows, and more art objects—many of them covered with glass domes—than Sarah could count. A great deal for their maid to have to dust!

During dinner Mr. Caulfield, after a bit of pompous bragging that the weekly *Star* was the best of the six daily and weekly newspapers in Leadville, finally turned his attention to Sarah. "Jeremy has told me that you are searching for your father," he said.

"Yes. Benjamin Lindley. Do you know him?" Sarah asked.

"Have you learned anything yet about your father?" Mr. Caulfield asked in turn, without answering Sarah's question.

"I learned only that Father had been in a gunfight," Sarah said. At the expression of surprise on Jeremy's face, she quickly added, "And he shot only in self-defense."

As Mr. Caulfield busied himself with his dinner, he asked, "Do you know the circumstances of the shooting?"

"No," Sarah said.

"I can help you there. Ben Lindley was at a poker table with a number of players, and he accused one of them of cheating. The unfortunate result of the gunfight was that the other man was shot through the heart, and Lindley ran away." He took another bite of roast, chewed it deliberately, and said, "I would like to know who told you that the shooting was in self-defense."

Not understanding why she was doing so, Sarah looked down at her plate and lied. "I don't remember."

"Perhaps it was one of Ben Lindley's friends. Just which of his friends have you spoken to?"

"I don't know who my father's friends are. I haven't

seen my father for ten years," Sarah said. "I arrived here knowing nothing about him, not even knowing where to start my search."

"But you must have spoken to someone in order to have the information that you just gave to me."

Sarah nodded, unsure how much she should tell, and what she wanted to keep to herself. Jeremy's uncle had promised to help her, so she had no reason to be so suspicious of him.

Sarah told about the visit to the Texas House and what Wilbur Owens had said to her, ignoring Jeremy's outbursts and complaints about what she had done.

"Obviously Owens wasn't the one who told you that the shooting was in self-defense," Mr. Caulfield said.

Sarah didn't answer.

Mr. Caulfield leaned back in his chair. "I hope you are right that self-defense was the reason," he said, "and if there are witnesses who will testify to this, it will certainly help his case." He paused and studied Sarah, who tried to keep her feelings from showing in her face. "Do you have any idea where your father might be staying?"

"No. I can only guess that he may be somewhere nearby."

His lips curved in a smile as he said, "Perhaps who-ever has been talking to you about your father could be persuaded to give you even more information. If we could find Ben Lindley and escort him back to Leadville, I'm sure we could quickly clear his name and make it possible for him to return to Chicago with you."

Mr. Caulfield's voice was so warm with hope and promise that Sarah cried out, "Oh! If it could only be!

I'm so eager to go home with him. I'm concerned about my sister and miss her so dreadfully much."

"Then please, my dear, come to me if you receive any news about your father. I promise to do my best to help."

"Thank you," Sarah answered.

She prepared herself for an after-dinner scolding from Jeremy, but when she was finally alone with him as he drove her home in his uncle's carriage, he didn't scold. He said, "Promise me that you won't go off on your own like that again."

"I can't promise you anything," Sarah said.

"At least you can allow me to go with you."

"You're busy working as a reporter, and I'm running out of time. I hope that Father has some money saved, but in case he hasn't, I need to find him while I still have enough left to buy our fares to Chicago."

"But I want to protect you, Sarah."

"I can protect myself," she said.

"With what?" He grinned. "Your umbrella?"

"I no longer have my umbrella. This afternoon a footpad stole the silver dollar I had in my purse and broke my umbrella—after I gave him two sound whacks with it."

Jeremy laughed so hard he nearly dropped the horse's reins. When he was finally able to talk, he said, "I wish I could have seen that. Never mind, Sarah. I'll buy you a new umbrella."

"Thank you," she said, but she began to wonder if maybe Clint hadn't been right. Maybe she would be safer if she carried her gun in her purse—not to shoot someone with, of course, but merely to frighten him.

Jeremy pulled the horse to a stop in front of Mrs. Hannigan's house. "I've convinced my uncle there should be items of literary merit in *The Star*," he said. "Theater in Leadville is thriving already and promises to be even better when Horace Tabor's opera house opens soon, so Uncle Chester's allowing me to review a performance of *Macbeth* at the Grand Central Theater. Will you accompany me tomorrow night?"

"Real theater?" Sarah, who avidly read about the plays appearing in Chicago, had only attended the theater twice. "Oh, Jeremy, I'd love to go!"

The next morning, after breakfast, Sarah followed the directions written on the paper Mrs. Hannigan had given her, and found the rooming house her father lived in. It was something like a hotel, with a desk in a narrow lobby, which was decorated only with a whitewash over the rough-cut walls.

Sarah approached the man in shirtsleeves and a vest who sat behind the desk, leaning on his elbows. "I am Miss Sarah Ann Lindley," she said. "My father is Benjamin Lindley, and I was told he rents a room here in this house."

Except for rolling his eyes to look up at her, the man didn't change positions. "Not anymore," he mumbled.

Sarah's heart sank. "Do you know where he moved?"

"Nope."

"You don't have an address—somewhere to deliver his things?"

"His belongin's are right here." The man lifted his chin only far enough to allow him to spit a brown stream of tobacco juice into a nearby brass spittoon.

"My father moved, but he left his possessions here?"

"I didn't say he moved," the man said. "He missed paying his rent two weeks in a row, and I got people wantin' the space, so I put his belongin's in a box and shoved it in the storeroom. It's not his room anymore."

What an aggravating man! Sarah tried to maintain a calm voice as she asked, "May I please have his belongings?"

"No matter to me," he said. He actually got to his feet, shuffled into the next room, and returned with a battered box.

Sarah took off the lid and looked inside at the few items that lay on the bottom of the box. "This is all he had?"

"All that's left. Somebody made off with the clothes."

Sarah picked up a silver-framed photograph of her mother—a young face so much like Susannah's that Sarah felt a catch in her throat.

"You may as well take that stuff," the man said. "Then I won't have to bother anymore with people who come here askin' about it."

Sarah was startled. "Who else saw these things?"

The man settled back into his chair, leisurely scratched his armpits, then propped his chin in the same position. "Some duded-up fellow a while back," he said. "Didn't ask his name. Didn't care."

"Did he take anything from the box?"

"Nope. He looked all through it but threw it back down. Wasn't too happy with what was there."

With an ache in her chest, Sarah glanced at the framed photograph, the worn book of poetry, and the few letters in her mother's handwriting. She put the lid on the box, picked it up, and left the rooming house. The poetry book she'd treasure just as Father must have, and the photograph of her mother she'd place on the table in her room where she could see it from her bed. *Someday soon, Father,* she promised, *I'll return them to you.*

Chapter 13

* * *

In the morning Sarah loaded her little derringer as Clint had taught her, squeamishly placed the gun in the bottom of her reticule, and left to see the marshal. Following directions given her by Mrs. Hannigan, she chose to walk down one of the side streets rather than the traffic-clogged boulevard, and she passed a number of dwelling places, some of them sturdy, some hastily thrown together, some of them nothing more than tents.

Ahead a small house was under construction, three carpenters hammering away at new lumber as they fastened supports to the frame that was already in place.

Suddenly a swarm of about eight men carrying axes and guns appeared at the opposite end of the block. They ran to the house under construction and began beating the workers. Two of the carpenters stayed and fought, but the third ran away. He raced toward Sarah, his face twisted in fear, as one of the thugs chased after him, brandishing a gun.

Sarah reached into her bag for her own gun. She could protect the carpenter and try to stop the man who was threatening him, but she shook so violently at the idea of actually using the gun to shoot someone that she was unable to wrap her fingers around the grip.

Fortunately the carpenter could move faster than his pursuer, so the man chasing him gave up and strode back, puffing and gulping air, to join the others. Three of the men chopped at the frame with their axes, demolishing it. They then threw the remaining two carpenters and the broken lumber into the street and began building another house, working as fast as possible.

People had come running, some of them crying, "Lot jumpers!" But as the original lot owners left the scene, the bystanders dispersed, a few of them carrying off the injured men, and soon the street was back to normal, with a new group of house builders the only difference.

Sarah, still horrified at what she'd witnessed, realized that a woman with a broom stood nearby in front of her tent. "What were those men doing?" Sarah asked her.

"Land in town is hard to come by," the woman said. "Small lots are selling for ten thousand dollars and more over on Chestnut. If you live on it, you own it. Those crooked lot jumpers are taking over Leadville."

"Can't anyone stop them?"

"In this town? I've heard from more than one source that some of the police are getting their share, and we have our doubts about some of the other lawmen hereabouts."

"What other lawmen?" Sarah asked, but the woman sighed, shook her head, threw open the flap over the doorway of her tent, and disappeared from sight.

With a shudder Sarah walked on, careful to cross the street when she had to pass the lot jumpers.

She made her way to Marshal Pat Kelly's office. Mrs. Hannigan had told her Marshal Kelly outranked both the sheriff and the local police force. She was confident about her mission until she walked into the room. All conversation ceased as a half dozen men turned to stare at her.

Sarah gritted her teeth as her cheeks grew hot, and she wished she could keep from blushing. She clutched her purse firmly and said, "I would like to speak to Marshal Kelly."

A husky, broad-shouldered man spoke up. "I'm Marshal Kelly, ma'am. What can I do for you?"

Sarah hesitated, glancing at the others in the room, all of whom kept watching until the marshal ordered, "Go about your own business. What the lady has to tell me is private." He held out a chair next to his desk and invited Sarah to sit down.

She poured out her story, telling him, "I need your help in finding my father."

"I know about the shooting," Marshal Kelly said. "There was some witnesses who first claimed it was self-defense, but they must have changed their minds. Your father's hidin' out for two reasons. One, I'd have to jail him on a murder charge until we could hold a trial. And two, the brother of the man Lindley shot is gunnin' for him."

Sarah gasped. "He's trying to kill my father?"

"That's about the size of it. Lindley accused Ezekiel Wulfe of cheatin' at poker. For all I know, Ezekiel did. He's a bad 'un, and I wouldn't put it past him. But family is family, and his brother Eli Wulfe is huntin' for Lindley, out to get revenge."

"I'm pretty sure my father is in this area," Sarah said.

"I think you're right about that," the Marshal told her. "This is rugged country, and there's only two ways out. If Lindley'd gone either by way of Weston Pass or Loveland Pass into Georgetown, he would have been seen."

"What are you going to do about it? How are you going to protect my father?" Sarah cried.

Marshal Kelly shook his head. "Leadville's run wild," he said. "There's no way I can protect even a portion of the law-abidin' folks hereabouts. Remember, your father's accused of murder. If he don't turn himself in, he'll just have to take care of himself."

As Sarah stood, she lifted her chin and stared down at the man with the law-enforcement badge pinned to his vest. "If you won't help him, I will," she said.

The Marshal heaved himself to his feet. "Take my advice, ma'am, and get out of this place. Go back where you came from."

Sarah didn't bother to answer as she turned and left the office. Of course she wouldn't go back. She had come here to find her father and bring him home, and she was determined to do so. If she had to help protect him in the bargain, she was ready for that, too.

She had tried her three sources: Mr. Caulfield's newspaper, records at the courthouse, and the marshal. The only one of the three who offered any hope or possibility was Mr. Caulfield.

She wished she could discuss the problem with Susannah. Susannah . . . Sarah longed to hear from her sister, but she knew that Susannah wouldn't receive Mrs. Hannigan's address for days and days—most likely weeks.

Sarah stopped short on Harrison Avenue, causing a near collision with two pedestrians, as it occurred to her that Susannah may have written to her care of general delivery. Yesterday, at the post office, she hadn't even thought to ask.

Sarah picked her way carefully over the uneven wooden sidewalk and tried not to be jostled by the crowd of pedestrians, but as she passed a nearby bank, someone called out to her, and she looked up to see Mr. Morton and Mr. Caulfield, who were so well dressed, they made quite a contrast to the people passing by.

It was Mr. Caulfield who had called to her. As she gladly stopped to say good morning, he made no attempt to introduce her to Mr. Morton. *He's aware that Mr. Morton and I have met,* Sarah thought. *They've obviously been talking about me.*

After they exchanged a few remarks about the weather turning cooler and a light snow expected, Mr. Morton asked, "Have you had any success in locating your father?"

"Unfortunately, no," Sarah said.

"I take it Marshal Kelly was no help?" Mr. Caulfield said.

Sarah took a quick breath. "How did you know I had gone to see the marshal?"

He smiled. "Jeremy told me that the marshal was one of the people you planned to speak to. You were walking from the direction of his office, so I made a guess. Was it correct?"

Sarah nodded. Obviously, in a town the size of Leadville, no matter what she did, Mr. Caulfield would learn about it. She answered, "Marshal Kelly told me that a man named Eli Wulfe is hunting for my father and wants to kill him."

Both Mr. Morton and Mr. Caulfield shook their heads sadly. "Naturally you want to reach your father first," Mr. Morton said. "We'll be glad to do anything we can to help you."

"Thank you," Sarah answered. "Most people I've talked to have told me to forget Father and go back to Chicago."

"They don't understand how you feel," Mr. Caulfield said.

"Who were these people?" Mr. Morton asked.

Sarah sighed. "The marshal, for one, and Lily, and"—Bessie's name came to mind, but the girl was so frightened, Sarah couldn't bring herself to speak it—"and even a footpad who robbed me," she added.

Neither man reacted to news of the footpad, as Sarah expected they would. Robberies must be so common that no one noticed or cared. Mr. Caulfield turned to Mr. Morton. "Lily?" he asked.

"She was on the stagecoach," Mr. Morton explained. "She usually plies her trade at the Texas House."

"Did she know your father well?" Mr. Caulfield asked Sarah.

"I think so," Sarah answered, and remembered Bessie's words. "My father risked his life to save Lily's, and she vowed she would always be grateful."

A woman came up to Mr. Morton, asking about her last bank deposit, and he bid good day to Sarah.

Mr. Caulfield tipped his hat and said, "It was a pleasure seeing you again. Violet and I look forward to your next visit to our home."

"Thank you," Sarah said. She was grateful for his support. He was a powerful man, and she just hoped he wasn't too hard a taskmaster for Jeremy.

At the post office Sarah found a letter had come for her, and she tore it open eagerly, unable to wait until she was home to read it. Seeing Susannah's bold, round handwriting made Sarah ache with eagerness to have all this behind her, to be home with Father and Susannah.

Sarah raced through the letter, then read it over more carefully. Susannah had written only two days after Sarah's departure, yet conditions at the boarding-house had worsened. Some of the boarders had begun complaining about the poorly cooked food and the miserly portions, and two had threatened to move.

Susannah reassured Sarah, however, that Mr. Abrams had promised he would not leave.

The last paragraph was filled with desperate pleas for Sarah to bring Father home soon, and Sarah could read Susannah's loneliness in the words. Susannah would be fifteen in mid-October, her birthday passing without Mother or Sarah to celebrate the day with her. No matter her brave words, Susannah was a child, a lonely child. Heartsick, Sarah wondered for a moment if it wouldn't be better to leave Leadville on the next stage.

I can't, she told herself. *I owe it to Susannah to stay and find Father and bring him home safely.*

Preoccupied with Susannah's letter as she walked down a side street on the way back to Mrs. Hannigan's, Sarah didn't realize that she was being followed until it was almost too late. Two men suddenly ran ahead of her, turned, and blocked her path. "Give us your money," one of them said.

Not again! Sarah thought.

"And be quick about it," the other one ordered.

Neither of them had pulled a gun. They were relying on frightening her. Two against one.

Sarah reached into her purse, wrapped her fingers around the grip on her gun, and pulled it out, aiming from one man to the other. "Put your hands on top of your head!" she ordered.

If she weren't so angry, she might have laughed at the expressions of astonishment and fear on their faces.

"Don't shoot us!" one of them said.

"You want our money, ma'am?" the other asked. "We'll give it to you."

"I don't want your money," Sarah said. "I want you to get out of here—fast!"

Backing away, tripping, they managed to turn and run down the street, weaving through the scattered pedestrians until they were out of sight.

At the boardinghouse Sarah offered to lend a hand with the mending or cooking. "It will help me sort out my problems if I stay busy," she said, so she tackled a stack of frayed collars that Mrs. Hannigan had promised to mend for her boarders.

The rhythmic in-and-out of the needle did prove to be a comfort to Sarah, and by the time she had finished, she had strengthened her resolve.

At supper she listened with interest to the tales the other boarders told about their jobs and the people they worked with. Mr. Vonachek informed them about the latest attempt to salt a failed mine with ore from some other place in order to sell it, and Elsie told a funny story about one of the younger children in her school. When she finished, Elsie sighed. She wished aloud that someone could be found who would fill the time left in her contract so that she could leave to be married.

The clock in the parlor chimed, and Sarah excused herself from the group. Susannah had packed her dark blue wool dress with the pearl buttons and satin trim around the neckline and cuffs. It would be perfect for a special occasion like the theater.

Sarah had read *Macbeth*, which was a good thing, because the audience made so much noise during the play, she would have had a hard time following it. Some of the miners became so involved, they shouted out advice and warnings, and one even pulled his gun, waving it at Lady Macbeth, before the stage manager was able to remove him.

"Don't let her get away with it!" he yelled.

When the play was over, and Jeremy and Sarah had left the theater, Sarah laughed and said, "I've never seen such an enthusiastic audience. In spite of all the noise, I enjoyed myself."

"Good," Jeremy said, "because in a few weeks the Tabor Opera House will have a grand opening, and I want you to go with me."

"A few weeks?" Sarah began to remind him that by that time surely she would have left Leadville, but she was interrupted by the excited voices of a crowd that had gathered in front of the nearby Texas House.

A man shoved his way out of the group and called to

his friend across the street. "Another murder," he shouted, "out in the alley." His eyebrows puckered into a worried frown. "But this time it was a woman," he said. "You know her. The dark-haired one named Lily."

Chapter 14

• • •

The people who gathered on Chestnut Street were hor-
rified, and during supper at Mrs. Hannigan's the next
day, some of the boarders spoke about their concern.
"Killing a woman in cold blood! With all the murders in
Leadville, killing a woman is practically unheard of,"
Mr. Vonachek said.

"If the people we've hired to enforce the law can't do
the job, then we should take the law into our own
hands," another boarder said.

"There's been a move to do that already," Mr.
Vonachek told him. "Haven't you heard of the Merchants Protective Patrol?"

"They can't supersede the law," Elsie warned.

"What law?" Mrs. Hannigan said.

"The criminal element must be stopped," Mr. Vonachek
argued.

Mrs. Hannigan put a hand on Sarah's shoulder. "You're
so pale, Sarah," she told her, "and you're not eating. Are
you not well? Would you like a cup of peppermint tea?"

"I'm upset about the murder," Sarah said. "I knew Lily." As everyone at the table looked up in shock, Sarah hurried to add, "She was one of the passengers on the stagecoach."

"You understand, I hope," Mrs. Hannigan said, "that a woman who lives as Lily did can expect nothing but trouble."

"But not murder," Sarah said.

"No," Mrs. Hannigan said slowly. "Not murder."

The door to the kitchen opened just a crack, and Mollie peeked through. As she caught Sarah's eye, she beckoned and quickly shut the door.

"Excuse me, please," Sarah said. "I'm really not hungry." She took her plate and hurried toward the kitchen.

The moment the door had shut, Mollie took the plate from Sarah's hands and whispered, "Go to the pantry. Bessie's there. She wants to talk to you."

Sarah did as Mollie instructed, and when she saw Bessie, she said, "I've already heard about Lily."

Bessie shook her head impatiently. "I didn't come to talk about Lily," she said. "I come because I been givin' thought to what you said about how I feel about my father and how you feel about yours. I've got two things to tell you."

She held up the palm of one hand as Sarah opened her mouth to speak. "Don't talk. Just listen. Part of what I want to say is that Ezekiel was actin' different durin' that poker game. I was servin' the drinks, and I noted right away that he seemed bent on pickin' a fight with Ben. It was as though he was lookin' for a chance to shoot him. Only it didn't work that way. Ezekiel drew first, but Ben shot first."

"Oh, thank you, Bessie," Sarah said. "If you'll testify to that—"

Again Bessie held up a hand. "Let me finish," she said. "The other thing I got to tell you is this. Not many people know this, but Ben had two good friends, a prospector name of Walter Fitch and his wife, Emma. Walter got killed last year when his ore wagon went over a cliff, but Emma got a job workin' nights in a bakery and stayed in Leadville. I think she and Walter are the only folks Ben ever trusted."

"Emma Fitch," Sarah said, memorizing the name. "Where does she live?"

"Don't ask me. You find her," Bessie said. "I've told you what I had to say, and I can't stay here any longer." She was out the pantry door and running across the yard before Sarah could stop her.

Sarah arrived at the courthouse the next morning soon after it opened. A fresh snowfall frosted the landscape, but the sky was thick and gray with the promise of more snow. With the mountain peaks invisible in the haze, Leadville had a grim, closed-in feeling.

Sarah pulled off her gloves and asked to see the property records. She thumbed through to the *F* section and quickly found the name of Fitch. The property was still under Walter Fitch's name, and the official numbered address was given. Sarah glanced at the other information written on the record, but she already had everything she needed.

The house was not far away—on Seventh Street— and the lot seemed to be about the eighth or ninth in from Harrison Avenue. Sarah knew she could find it.

As she pulled on her gloves, preparing to leave the

courthouse, the door swung open and Jeremy stepped inside. His eyes shone as he saw her.

"Sarah!" he said. "You can help me with a story. Uncle Chester wants to do a lead story about lot jumpers, and he sent me to go through the records and take notes. We're going to match names with property and try to make our readers aware of what must be done to stop these ruffians."

Sarah smiled at the enthusiasm in Jeremy's voice. *Our* newspaper, he had said. Apparently, in spite of the hard work, he was enjoying his apprenticeship.

"I wish I could help you, but I can't," she told him. "I've found the name of one of my father's close friends, and now that I know where she lives, I'm going to talk to her."

Jeremy bristled, unconsciously moving between Sarah and the door. "It's not in a place like the Texas House, is it?" he demanded.

"No," she said. "The person I'm going to see is a woman named Emma Fitch. She works in a bakery and lives in a home on Seventh Street."

"Do you want me to go with you?"

"No, thank you. You have your job to do, and it looks as though it's going to take you a long time."

Jeremy put a hand on Sarah's shoulder and looked down on her with so much affection that her heart gave a little jump. Dear, kind Jeremy. For an instant she impulsively rested her cheek against his hand.

He moved closer. "May I come by this evening and see you?" he asked.

"Yes," Sarah answered.

Slowly, reluctantly, Jeremy removed his hand from

her shoulder. "In the meantime," he said, "please, Sarah, don't go anywhere that might be dangerous." He smiled and added, "At least not until I get you another umbrella."

If Jeremy only knew that I carry a handgun in my purse! Sarah thought. She waved good-bye, stepped carefully down the slippery steps, and headed for Seventh Street.

The Fitch house was a small square cabin with clay packed between the logs, set back from the others along the street. Sarah made her way down the snow-covered walk and knocked at the front door.

She waited a few moments, listening to the perpetual sounds of Leadville: someone's off-key singing, the rumble of carts and wagons, and the unceasing background noise of thousands of humans and animals cooped up in a relatively small space. If Mrs. Fitch worked nights in the bakery, surely she'd be home by now. Sarah knocked again, this time pounding on the door.

In a moment a woman opened the door. Her dark hair was loosely braided down her back, and she clutched a faded, red-flannel wrapper around her nightgown. Her eyes were slightly swollen with sleep. "What do you want?" she began, but her expression changed as she took a hard look at Sarah.

"Who are you?" she asked, but Sarah could see sudden recognition in the woman's eyes, even though they'd never met. Mrs. Fitch knew Ben Lindley. She had seen him in his child.

"I'm Sarah Ann Lindley. May I please come in and talk to you about my father?"

For only an instant the woman looked frightened.

Then she composed herself, opened the door, and stood aside so that Sarah could enter.

Although the outside of the house was rough and unattractive, the parlor was warm and cozy with comfortable chairs grouped around an iron potbellied stove. Doilies decorated the arms and backs of the chairs and the small tables, and the oil lamps were hand painted with sprays of roses and forget-me-nots. As though the mountain peaks that ringed the town were not enough, a large painting of mountains hung on the far wall against a cheerful wallpaper sprigged with flowers.

"Mrs. Fitch, I was told that you are my father's closest friend," Sarah said. "My mother has died, and I came to find Father and take him home."

"Leave your father alone," Mrs. Fitch said.

"I can't. My younger sister, Susannah, is waiting for us to return."

Mrs. Fitch sat in the nearest chair, and Sarah perched on the edge of a chair across from her. "Please help me," Sarah begged.

"Go home, now, and maybe your father will be able to join you later, when it's safe for him to do so," Mrs. Fitch told her.

"Why can't he come forward now? We have a witness who will testify that he shot in self-defense."

The corners of Mrs. Fitch's mouth twisted down in bitterness. "No one would dare to testify to that."

"But it's the truth!"

"Since when has the truth mattered?"

"Mrs. Fitch," Sarah said, "there are influential people in town who want to help Father."

Stubbornly Mrs. Fitch shook her head.

"If we can get Father out of Leadville, he can't be harmed."

Mrs. Fitch didn't answer.

Sarah waited a moment, then asked, "Do you know where my father is?"

Again Mrs. Fitch remained silent, her lips pressed into a tight, hard line.

Sarah got to her feet. "I hoped you would help me. At the moment I don't know who else can, but I'm not giving up. I'm going to keep searching until I find Father."

Mrs. Fitch jumped up, the sides of her wrapper flapping open. She tugged it together, as though it could protect her, and snapped, "You're a little fool. Hasn't it occurred to you that if you knew where your father was and let it be known, you could lead the way for those who want to kill him?"

Sarah was momentarily confused. "You mean Eli Wulfe?"

"Get out of here!" Mrs. Fitch ordered. She stomped to the door and threw it open. "Out! And don't come back!"

With what dignity she had left, Sarah swept past Mrs. Fitch and left the house, but as she started down the walk, Mrs. Fitch called to her, anger drained from her voice. "If you love your father, Sarah, then please leave Leadville. Please."

This time Sarah didn't answer. Of course she loved her father, and if she knew where he was, she'd take steps to protect him. She was tired of people simply ordering her away. Feeling Mrs. Fitch's eyes burning into her back, Sarah lifted her chin a notch higher and quickly walked back to Mrs. Hannigan's.

She found her landlady in a dreadful state. An apron covering her ample middle, strands of hair flying awry from the bun at the back of her neck, Mrs. Hannigan trotted out of the kitchen muttering under her breath, but she stopped when she saw Sarah. "That Mollie," Mrs. Hannigan said. "She's gone without a by-your-leave. Disappeared. Even left dirty dishes on the drain board last night."

"What happened to her?" Sarah asked. She remembered Bessie running across the yard. Had Mollie run after her?

"If I knew, I'd tell you," Mrs. Hannigan answered. "I went to her home this morning to inquire, and her whole family had moved out—father, mother, and five children. Already there were squatters takin' over the house and furniture."

"You mean they left Leadville?" Sarah was shaken. Bessie was going to be her witness as to what had really happened.

"Looks that way."

Mrs. Hannigan started past Sarah, but Sarah stopped her by placing a hand on her arm. "Wait," Sarah said, as an idea took shape. "You need household help, and I'm well experienced in running a boardinghouse. I'm a good cook, too."

"You? But you're a paying guest here."

"Mrs. Hannigan," Sarah said, "I know now that it's going to take longer to find my father than Susannah and I had thought. If I don't begin to earn wages, I'm going to run out of money. I'd greatly appreciate the job."

Mrs. Hannigan pinched her chin between her thumb

and forefinger and began to think, humming a tuneless sound to herself. Finally she said, "It postpones my hunting for a new girl to help out, but I like you, Sarah, and I think we can make it work. How about if you take on Mollie's chores in exchange for room and board?"

"Thank you," Sarah answered, grateful that at least she'd now have the means to stay in Leadville. "I'll run up the back stairs and change my clothes and get right to work."

Jeremy was astonished and somewhat displeased when he found that Sarah was working as a maid.

"And a cook," she said as she put the last of the clean supper dishes in the cupboard. "I know how to do this job well, so why shouldn't I take it? Besides, while I'm scrubbing floors or scraping carrots, it gives me a chance to think."

"But a job should be fun," Jeremy told her.

She smiled. "Like being a reporter?"

"For now," he said, "until I get tired of it." He chuckled. "And then I think I'll write a book. An adventure novel about a young newspaper reporter in Leadville. Or maybe in Oregon. I haven't made up my mind whether Oregon or California is where I'll travel next."

Sarah reached around Jeremy to wipe down the drainboard, but he circled her waist and tipped up her chin. "But not alone. With you, Sarah," he said, and kissed her.

His lips on hers were light and warm and loving. Sarah, who'd never been kissed, caught her breath in shock, then, to her surprise, found herself responding. It was only when she heard the kitchen door opening

147

that she jumped back, once more in control of her senses, and began to furiously scrub the drainboard.

"Don't, Jeremy," she said, as soon as the intruding boarder had poured a glass of water for himself and left. "I can't let anyone make me forget what my purpose is here."

Whether or not Jeremy paid attention, Sarah didn't know. His eyes danced with mischief, and he grinned.

Sarah kept her purpose in mind. She worked hard over the next few days, redoing some of the chores Mollie had done halfheartedly, and by late afternoon that Thursday, she had shopped for Mrs. Hannigan and had a brisket of beef seasoned and simmering for supper. She was shocked at the high prices she'd been charged. Ten cents a pound for the beef, five cents a pound for the potatoes, and forty-five cents a pound for coffee! As for eggs, vegetables, and fruits—there were none available.

With at least an hour before it would be time to peel potatoes and prepare the rest of the meal, Sarah hung up her apron and hurried up the back stairs to change into a skirt and shirtwaist. She pulled on her coat, scarf, boots, bonnet, and gloves. Darkness was already falling, but the sky had cleared, and there would be a full moon that night. During the day, as she worked, one thought kept returning. She must see Mrs. Fitch. Sarah had found out no more about her father since her visit with that woman. She was certain Mrs. Fitch knew exactly where he was. Sarah had to change Mrs. Fitch's mind about letting her know, too. If Sarah was lucky, Mrs. Fitch wouldn't have left her home yet to go to the bakery.

When Sarah arrived at Mrs. Fitch's house, she raised a hand to knock, but the door was ajar.

"Mrs. Fitch!" she called. She waited for an answer, then pushed the door open.

The fire in the stove had gone out, and the room was freezing, but there was enough daylight still left to see that everything in the room was broken and torn. The framed painting had been smashed, the stuffing from the furniture pulled out in great, wadded tufts, and the tables reduced to splinters. Torn strips of wallpaper dangled from the walls.

Because of the clutter, it took a moment longer for Sarah to recognize the body of the woman who lay under some of the rubble.

When she did, Sarah clung to the door frame and screamed.

Chapter 15

• ◆ •

People on the street came running. A policeman arrived . . . or was he a deputy sheriff? Sarah didn't know. She groped through a nightmare, hoping to wake up. Someone demanded, "Stop screaming," and slapped her, shocking her into silence; then someone else moved her away from the crowd and sat her down, saying, "Drink this, miss. You'll feel better."

Whatever it was tasted vile, burned her throat, and made her cough, but Sarah recovered enough to answer questions. As soon as the lawman said she could, she turned and ran all the way back to Mrs. Hannigan's house.

Sobbing loudly, Sarah had just rounded the corner at Fifth Street when she heard a voice call her name and running footsteps thud toward her.

Someone gripped Sarah's shoulders and flung her around. She looked up, so grateful to see Clint that she sagged against him.

"Sarah! What happened to you? Tell me!" His voice

cracked, and Sarah could hear the fear in it—fear for her.

"Oh, Clint!" she cried, sobbing even harder. "A woman was murdered! And it's my fault!"

Clint put an arm around Sarah and walked her from the moonlight and the pedestrian traffic into the darkness and privacy of a nearby porch. He took off Sarah's bonnet and stroked back her hair, comforting and soothing her, until she was able to tell him everything that had happened.

"You can't blame yourself," he told her.

"But I have to. The man who's after Father—I must have led him to Mrs. Fitch."

"Who else knew that Mrs. Fitch was your father's close friend?"

"Only a waitress named Bessie, that I know of."

"Maybe Bessie had a hand in it."

"But she's left Leadville."

"You may not have been the only one Bessie told. And there's something else to think about. It's likely the crime didn't have anything to do with your father or you. Plenty of robberies take place around here. It's not usual for a woman to get shot during a robbery, but it can happen. Crime in Leadville is getting worse all the time."

"Oh, Clint." Sarah sighed with relief. "I'm glad you're here."

As she looked up into his face, Clint's arms wrapped tightly around her, and his mouth came down on hers. His kiss was tender, but so strong and intent that Sarah trembled, and her heart began to pound.

She didn't want the kiss to end, but when it did, she

pulled away from Clint, staggered back a step, and took a long, shuddering breath to steady herself. "You understand, don't you, Clint, that when I find Father I'm taking him back to Chicago?" she asked.

He nodded solemnly. "I want you to do whatever pleases you, Sarah."

"Right now," she said, finding it hard to pull her gaze away from his, "I want to go back to Mrs. Hannigan's."

Everyone at the boardinghouse was upset when Sarah told her story. "A woman like Lily—that's one thing," Mrs. Hannigan said, "but a respectable woman getting herself murdered? Well, I shake in my boots to think of what this town's come to!"

As Mr. Vonachek began to talk about the organization of the Merchants Protective Patrol, which had grown to at least seven hundred strong, and their aim to chase off the worst of the bad element in town, Sarah hurried up the back stairs to her room, changed to her working clothes, and came down to finish the preparations for supper.

Because it would be difficult for the serving girl to sit in the dining room with the boarders, Sarah served them the meal and ate in the kitchen as soon as everyone else had finished and the plates were cleared away. Clint waited and ate with Sarah. He finished a large second helping, pushed back his chair, and said, "You're a mighty good cook, too."

"Too?"

"On top of everything else."

His smile was so warm, his eyes so blue, that Sarah's knees wobbled. Quickly she took their plates to the drainboard and scraped them.

Before Sarah realized what was happening, Clint had lifted the kettle of hot water from the top of the stove and poured it into a basin, adding soft lye soap and a stack of dirty dishes. "I'll wash," he said.

"But that's *my* job," Sarah said.

"I was taught that if a job needs doing, do it. That's the way it is in ranching. Everybody lends a hand."

"I wouldn't be much help on a ranch. I don't know the first thing about raising cattle," Sarah teased.

"It wouldn't be cattle I'd ask you to raise," Clint countered, and Sarah busied herself with drying plates, hoping he wouldn't see the blush that burned her cheeks.

During the night Sarah slept fitfully as a nagging thought broke into her scattered, terrifying dreams about Mrs. Fitch. It reminded her that there was something else about Mrs. Fitch she should know, something else that Sarah hadn't paid enough attention to.

"What is it?" Sarah asked aloud as she struggled awake in the early gray-streaked morning and sat up in bed.

The answer rushed into her mind. Mrs. Fitch's property records. The house on Seventh Street wasn't the only property the Fitches had owned. There was something about a mine. A description of the location of a mine. If the Fitches had owned and worked a mine— even though now it was a failed, abandoned one—there'd be a shack on the property—a place where someone could hide out and not be discovered.

Sarah was so excited that her hands shook as she dressed, and twice she dropped the pins from her hair, which spilled around her shoulders. She forced herself to slow down, to breathe normally and dress carefully.

She'd make a return trip to the courthouse as soon as she'd completed the most demanding of her chores.

It was not until after dishes from the noon dinner had been cleared away that Sarah was able to take some free time. She tucked her derringer into her purse, hurried to the courthouse, and once again asked to see the records she needed. There was no record of any kind of land or property in Benjamin Lindley's name, but Walter Fitch had owned a mine, *The Emma Bee*. A description of the property was given, with its location, out beyond Fryer Hill, and a notation that the mine was no longer in production.

The Emma Bee. Sarah laughed at the name, which had set a thousand questions buzzing in her head: Should she try to go there today? Maybe tomorrow would be better. She could arrange with Mrs. Hannigan to take some time off. Or would it be better not to tell Mrs. Hannigan what she was planning?

Suppose she found Father? Sarah tried to think of what to do next. If Father were at the shack, how would she manage to get him back to Leadville and out of town? With Clint's help? Maybe Clint could smuggle Father onto the stagecoach. She knew she could count on Clint. But tomorrow Clint wouldn't be in Leadville. Today was his day off, and he'd be driving the stage back to Denver tomorrow. Sarah couldn't wait for tomorrow. She'd have to go today.

Her head ached. There was too much to think about. Maybe this would be nothing more than a wild-goose chase. What was she to do?

Panic won't help, Sarah reminded herself. *Take this step by step.* She'd check out the cabin at the mine. If the cabin was empty, Sarah would simply return to Mrs. Hannigan's and begin preparations for supper. If she found Father there, they could work out a plan—the two of them together. Yes. She liked that idea.

Oh, Father, Sarah thought, *I can't wait to see you! I've missed you for such a long, long time.*

She jumped as Jeremy stepped up beside her and tilted his head to peer into her face. "What are you dreaming about, Sarah? I said hello, and you didn't hear me."

"I'm sorry," Sarah said.

"For that matter, what are you doing back here at records? Looking up lot jumpers is my job, not yours." He took the papers from her hands and glanced at them with a puzzled frown. "Fitch? Sarah, haven't you heard what happened to Mrs. Fitch?"

"Yes," Sarah said. "I have."

She tried to look impassive, but Jeremy studied her a moment and said, "Sarah, the expression on your face gives you away. Do you know what it tells me? You've discovered something. It's about your father, isn't it?"

"Hush," she said, and glanced quickly around, thankful that no one had been close enough to overhear. But Jeremy read the description of the Fitch property holdings, and his eyes shone with excitement.

"An abandoned mine?" he whispered. "Do you think your father's there?"

"Be quiet! No one must know."

Jeremy's eyebrows dipped into a frown. "You're not planning to go there alone, are you? I won't allow it."

"You have nothing to say about it," Sarah told him. "Whatever I do is my own decision."

"No," Jeremy insisted. "You can't ride into the mountains alone. I'm going with you."

It was pointless to argue with him. Someone might overhear. "Very well," she said. She took the records from Jeremy's hands, returned them to their place, and closed the lid on the box.

Her quick acquiescence took him by surprise. "When are you planning to go?"

"Tomorrow," she said. "Early in the morning."

"I'll get horses for us."

"Thank you."

Jeremy's eyes narrowed as he studied Sarah. "You're giving in too easily."

She shrugged. "It would do no good to argue."

"That's true enough," Jeremy said. He smiled at Sarah, but she didn't return the smile. She solemnly said goodbye to Jeremy and left the courthouse.

By the time she reached the sidewalk, her mind was made up. She'd go to Father now. Her treatment of Mrs. Hannigan would be no better than Mollie's had been, but she had no choice.

Clint had said she could use his mare anytime she wished. Now was the time. Sarah walked directly to the stables and arranged to have Lady saddled.

Samson was still stabled, and Sarah looked around nervously as she waited for Lady to be brought. She didn't want to meet Clint. Much as she would love to have his company—and Jeremy's—she had to go to Father alone.

Sarah rode out of town through the traffic leisurely, as though this were nothing more than a pleasure ride, up to Seventh Street and west on Seventh. As she passed Mrs. Fitch's house, she shuddered, but she kept going. The street became a road, which for a little while wound through rolling hills. Ore wagons rumbled past, and people on foot and on horseback traveled in both directions.

Sarah occasionally glanced back, trying to discover if she was being followed; but all the men she saw looked the same, with dusty clothes and dusty faces, as they plodded toward the mines or toward town. Twice as the traffic thinned she branched off on one of the narrow side roads that led toward mine sites, and no one followed her; so when Sarah reached the crossroad she was searching for, she was confident that she would cause no danger to her father.

The names of mines were printed on scraps of wood and tacked on a pole: *Golden Fortune, Little Betty, Silver Baby.* Among them were the faded words: *The Emma Bee.* Sarah clucked to Lady and dug a heel into her side. As the horse obediently moved forward, Sarah guided her up the narrow lane and into the mountains.

The Emma Bee was the last of the mines that had been posted. It was carved into a hollow against the side of a rise. As Sarah had hoped, there *was* a shack back among the trees, and as she watched, a wisp of smoke lifted from its chimney.

Father! You're here! I knew you would be!

Sarah spurred Lady on, reining her in near the cabin door. She jumped from the saddle and tied the reins to a branch of the nearest tree.

Almost too late Sarah realized that her father would be wary of visitors and might meet anyone who approached with gunshot. "Father!" she called. "Don't be afraid. It's me. It's your daughter, Sarah."

The door opened, and she could see the figure of a man standing back in the shadows. "Sarah?" he asked.

With a cry of joy, Sarah ran into the cabin.

Chapter 16

• • •

She stopped short as she entered the cabin. The man who faced her, rifle in hand, was not her father. He was gaunt with dark rings under his eyes and hollows in his cheeks. His beard was unkempt, his hair was matted, and he smelled of sweat. He smelled of fear.

Never taking his eyes from Sarah, he gave a push to the door, which swung shut with a bang. He took two long steps toward her and pulled her bonnet back from her face.

Sarah gasped but held her ground, though she was sure he could hear the loud, frightened thumping of her heart. How could she have been so stupid, blundering into a lonely place like this? She would never get out. Even though she was terrified, she tried to make plans. She'd slowly edge toward the door. The man had a gun, but if she could take him by surprise . . . She gripped her purse. Well, for that matter, she had a gun, too.

She tried to keep her voice even as she said, "I'm

sorry, I made a mistake. I'm looking for my father, Benjamin Lindley."

"Oh, Sarah," the man said. "I *am* your father."

Ben laid the gun on the table, and he and Sarah faced each other, suddenly shy. " 'She walks in beauty like the night, of cloudless climes and starry skies,' " he murmured. "Sarah, you have become such a beautiful young woman."

Hearing her father recite Lord Byron's words warmed Sarah as nothing else could have. How well she remembered the poems he once had read to her.

"How is your mother?" he asked. "How is little Susannah?"

Sarah hadn't thought of how she'd break the news to her father. There must be a gentle way, but at the moment it escaped her. "I'm sorry, Father," she said. "Mother died two months ago."

It had been such a long time since Father had been home, such a long time since his last letter; yet his face crumpled like a wad of discarded paper, and tears ran down his cheeks. "Margaret, Margaret," he murmured over and over to himself.

Sarah no longer hesitated. She ran forward and wrapped her arms around her father, holding and comforting him as he cried. He was so thin his shoulder bones felt sharp and knobby, and the strong, muscular arms she remembered had become weak and soft. Sarah wept, too, not for her mother this time, but for her father.

Finally Ben stepped back and tried to dry his face on a dirty shirtsleeve. Sarah reached into her purse and handed him a clean handkerchief. "Father," she said, "I've come to bring you home."

She briefly told him about what Uncle Amos and Aunt Cora were up to, and she reassured him that she knew why he was in hiding. "And I know that you shot in self-defense," she said.

"It makes no difference," he told her. "They'll never let me leave Leadville alive."

"I know people who will protect you from Eli Wulfe."

"Protect me? Eli's only the executioner."

"I don't understand what you're saying."

Ben shook his head sadly, and for a moment she saw the familiar spark of love and fun in his eyes. "Sarah, my little dreamer, I regret the years I spent away from you. I wish I could make up for them now, but I can't."

"Mother called me a dreamer, too," Sarah told him, "but I'm not—at least I no longer am. I've discovered that I'm a woman who can make decisions and plans and carry them out. I was able to come for you and find you."

"When your mother called you a dreamer, she didn't mean it was a bad thing to be."

"Father, I heard the disapproval in her voice."

"Oh, Sarah, believe me, you don't have to give up your dreams in order to become a mature, responsible person." He sighed. "You can't be *only* a dreamer, chasing unrealistic dreams that are always at a distance. You can be happy with the smaller dreams that can be within your reach. But you must have some dreams to cherish, or you'll end up living a life without joy."

Isn't that what your dreams have brought you? Sarah thought, and guiltily she turned away so her father couldn't see her face.

But she was not quick enough. "Unfortunately, I'm

afraid I spent much of my life chasing unrealistic, out-of-reach dreams," her father said in a voice choked with sorrow.

Sarah reached out a hand to take one of his. "Why did you leave us, Father? I missed you so terribly much! And Mother missed you. She kept each of your letters and read them over and over again."

"I wanted to try the West," he explained. "I don't expect you to understand, but in Chicago I was smothering in a dull, low-paying office clerk's job, and in the West there was great opportunity. I asked Margaret to come with me, and I wrote to her several times—from Kansas City, from Denver, and when I arrived in Leadville—telling her how lonely I was for my family and begging her to bring you and Susannah. But each time her answer was the same. It was nonsense to take chances, she said, when you could have your feet firmly and safely planted in one place."

"I can almost hear Mother saying that," Sarah murmured.

"I always intended to go back to my family someday," Ben said. "I'd be rich and arrive with my arms filled with gifts. Margaret would be overjoyed. You and Susannah would run to me with outstretched arms."

His expression became so filled with misery that Sarah wondered if he was going to cry again, but he added, "And now it's too late. My dreams have come to an end."

"No," Sarah told him. "Please don't say that."

"It's just a matter of time, Sarah. 'Death lays his icy hand on kings; sceptre and crown must tumble down, and in the dust be equal made with the poor crooked scythe and spade.' "

"Don't!" Sarah cried. "Listen to me, Father. I'm going to take you back to Chicago."

For the first time she thought she saw hope in his face.

"And I promise I'm going to clear your name."

He pulled his hand away from hers and walked to the far side of the room. "It's not that simple."

"You killed that man in self-defense."

When he didn't answer, Sarah asked, "There's more, isn't there? When I mentioned Eli Wulfe's name, you said he was only the executioner. That means someone else is involved. Tell me the rest, Father. I'll need to know if I'm going to help you."

"No one can help me, Sarah," he began. "I brought this on myself." He walked back and forth speaking in a low voice, as though he were talking to himself and not to Sarah. "It was my own fault. My dream hadn't come true, and I thought of other ways to reach it. I'd discovered a crime that was taking place. I should have stopped them . . . gone to the authorities . . . to Pinkerton's. They wouldn't be corrupted. . . . But I thought how they'd pay me to keep the knowledge to myself. It was like an insurance policy. If I let them know I had the proof and had hidden it where they'd never find it, that would be enough to insure my safety."

Sarah winced at the bitterness in her father's laugh. "Let's go home to Chicago," she pleaded. "You'll be fine, Father, once we get you out of this horrible place with its footpads and lot jumpers."

He turned, his eyes wide and burning as he stared at

her. "Those criminals are nothing, Sarah. The greatest robberies in Leadville are being committed by a few people who are stealing from others in a hidden, even more vicious way. And I learned about it. I'm to blame, too, for trying to protect myself instead of making it known."

"Who are you talking about?" she asked. "What are these people doing?"

Ben had no chance to answer. The door suddenly slammed open, and a large-boned, heavyset man stomped into the room.

"Eli," Ben said, and the defeat in his voice caused Sarah to cry out.

"Father! I did this to you! He must have followed me!"

Eli's laugh was more of a grunt. "I didn't have to," he said, and with one hand he shoved Sarah so hard that she stumbled backward and fell. "Stay there," he ordered as he kept his eyes on Ben, "and keep quiet."

"Eli," Ben said, "I'm unarmed." His glance flicked toward the rifle on the table, but it was out of reach.

"Makes no difference."

"Your brother was armed, and I shot him only in self-defense. He drew first."

Slowly, hoping Eli wouldn't notice the movement, Sarah slipped her hand inside the purse that still hung from her left arm.

"You won't have that chance," Eli said.

Sarah's fingers curled around the grip on her derringer.

Eli pulled his gun from the holster that rode low on his hip and brought it up, but as he did, Sarah whipped her handgun from the purse, cocked it, aimed it in Eli's direction, and pulled the trigger.

The sound of the double explosion ricocheted through the cabin, slamming against Sarah's ears. She saw a wisp of smoke coming from Eli's gun as he staggered back against the door frame, clutching his shoulder. She aimed and shot again.

As Eli whirled and ran from the doorway, Sarah turned toward her father, who was sprawled on the floor. She started toward him, but he raised himself on one elbow and grunted, "Sarah! Take cover! Turn the table on end. Get behind it before Eli comes back!"

But Sarah froze. She had seen blood on Eli's shoulder, and there was blood on her father's chest—red blood, dark blood that spilled through his fingers, over his shirt, and onto the floor.

On her hands and knees, she crawled and scrambled toward her father. As she gently lifted her father's head and shoulders onto her lap, Sarah heard shouts and the sound of hoofbeats. "You're going to be all right," she soothed. "Someone's coming. They'll help you, Father."

"Sarah," he said, "I'm sorry . . . I . . ."

"Listen to me," she said, "The people who had you shot should be punished. And you said the robberies they're committing are hurting other people. Now's your chance to make amends, Father, and to clear your own name."

He coughed for a moment, unable to speak, and Sarah winced at the blood that ran down his chin.

"If you can't do it, I will. I promise, Father! I promise! Where is this proof you spoke about? Where have you hidden it?"

Ben fell back, sighing and closing his eyes, and Sarah cried out in panic, "Father! Please don't die!"

165

His fingertips touched hers, and he whispered, "Remember . . . your mother . . . Margaret . . ."

Sarah could hear running footsteps, and she cried out, "Help us! Please, help us!"

Jeremy staggered into the doorway and held onto the door frame, panting and trying to catch his breath. "Sarah!" he gasped.

"Jeremy!" Sarah cried. "My father was shot. He needs help!"

Clint appeared in the doorway and shoved past Jeremy, dropping to his knees beside Sarah and her father.

"Help him," she begged, but she heard the hollow rattle of air in her father's lungs, and she knew it was too late.

"I'm sorry, Sarah," Clint murmured. He gently lifted her father's body from her arms and laid him on the cabin floor. He took a firm grip on Sarah's arms and helped her to her feet.

For just an instant she closed her eyes and swayed, and when she opened them, Clint was supporting one of her arms, Jeremy the other.

"We got Marshal Kelly to come with us as soon as we realized where you had gone," Jeremy told her. "We saw Eli Wulfe riding from the cabin and thought we could catch him."

"You didn't?"

"The marshal's still trailing him." Jeremy glanced at Clint. "Barnes here was at Mrs. Hannigan's looking for you when I arrived. He knew you'd taken his horse out, and I guessed you'd probably gone to the mine. Why didn't you wait, Sarah? You could have been killed, too. If your father hadn't been able to wound Wulfe, and if Wulfe hadn't heard us coming—"

"Father didn't shoot Eli," Sarah said. She glanced from the small derringer, which lay on the floor, to Clint's face. "*I* shot him," she said. "I didn't believe that I could ever bring myself to shoot a man, but I had to try to stop him from killing my father."

"*You* shot him?" Jeremy looked incredulous, but Clint nodded with understanding.

"It probably kept him from killing you, too," he said.

Sarah tried not to look at her father's body on the floor. She felt hollow inside, too heartbroken even to cry. "Father wasn't the same as I'd pictured him in my mind," she said. "For that matter I can't even remember the Sarah I used to be. Everything has changed, and I'm someone else."

"That's the way of it," Clint told her. "Life keeps changing. It happens to everybody."

"The old Sarah has come to an end," Sarah murmured. "The new Sarah is beginning."

She glanced down at her bloodstained clothing, and her mind began whirling with all the things she must do. "I have to go back," she said.

Jeremy stepped closer and placed his other hand on her shoulder, and her fingers felt the sudden pressure from Clint's hand.

"Don't leave Leadville," Jeremy said.

"Sarah . . ." Clint began.

Sarah shook her head. "Back to Mrs. Hannigan's," she said firmly. "To begin with I have to arrange for a proper funeral for Father, and I must reach Susannah. I've decided to stay in Leadville, and I'm going to send for Susannah to join me."

She looked from Clint to Jeremy. They'd both helped her face so much, but now they couldn't know what she had to do. She saw the light in both pairs of eyes, but she couldn't stop to think about that now.

Jeremy was the first to speak. "What about your home in Chicago?" he asked. "It's your property. Are you going to let your relatives just take it over?"

"As Clint reminded us, life keeps changing. That doesn't matter," Sarah replied emphatically. She managed the hint of a smile for Clint.

They think I want to stay in Leadville, Sarah thought, *and yet I'd like nothing more than to be free to go home to Chicago.*

What Father had told her was a secret. She must keep it to herself until she could find the proof he'd hidden. His murderers had robbed her of her father, and she burned with passion to hunt them out. She'd find them and force them to face justice.

She had promised her father she would do it. She had promised to clear his name. Her life wouldn't be her own until she kept her promise.

And promises were made to be kept.

About the Author

JOAN LOWERY NIXON is the acclaimed author of more than eighty fiction and nonfiction books for children and young adults. She is a three-time winner of the Mystery Writers of America Edgar Award and the recipient of many Children's Choice awards. Her popular books for young adults include The Orphan Train Quartet, *A Family Apart, Caught in the Act, In the Face of Danger,* and *A Place to Belong,* as well as the Hollywood Daughters trilogy, *Star Baby, Overnight Sensation,* and *Encore.* She was moved by the true experiences of the children on the nineteenth-century orphan trains to research and write The Orphan Train Quartet.

Mrs. Nixon and her husband live in Houston, Texas.

Follow Sarah Lindley's further adventures
in the upcoming companion volume,
A Deadly Promise.

Sarah took a closer look at the man who had come to dance with her. She had seen those eyes and heavy eyebrows before. Where? Suddenly she remembered. This man had stared at her over a dirty bandanna mask as he'd helped rob the train Sarah and Jeremy had taken from St. Louis to Kansas City. And that voice. She'd never forget it. This man had tossed a silver dollar to the conductor on the Missouri Pacific train and called, "Have a drink on Jesse James!"

"You're not Jesse James either," Sarah blurted.

"You remembered?" He grinned. "I like to have my fun."

Sarah took a step backward. "Who are you? What are you doing here?"

The music began, and the man nodded in what could have passed for a bow. "My name's Harley Emmett, and I'm stayin' only long enough for one dance, no more, no less. It's worth a hundred dollars to me just to dance with the lady who took a shot at Eli Wulfe."